SOMETHING WAS WRONG

"There's something very odd about the atmosphere on this ship this evening," George said. "Miss Seeton agrees with me."

"Stop looking around you so furtively, sit down and tell us what is going on."

"Oh, very well. You're bound to find out pretty soon anyway. I was just wondering how to put it, as a matter of fact. You know that bounder Witley?"

"Really, George!" said Meg. "Of all the idiotic questions—"

"Course you do. Silly of me to ask. Well, he's, um, well, not to put too fine a point on it, dead, actually."

"Oh, dear, I had a feeling that this day would end badly," Miss Seeton said, not sounding in the least surprised. "I was quite unable to achieve the proper frame of mind for my yoga practice . . ."

MISS SEETON
AT THE HELM

HAMPTON CHARLES

BERKLEY BOOKS, NEW YORK

MISS SEETON AT THE HELM

A Berkley Book / published by arrangement with
the author and the estate of Heron Carvic

PRINTING HISTORY
Berkley edition / September 1990

ISBN: 0-425-12264-6

A BERKLEY BOOK® TM 757,375
Berkley Books are published by The Berkley Publishing Group,
200 Madison Avenue, New York, New York 10016.
The name ''BERKLEY'' and the ''B'' logo
are trademarks belonging to Berkley Publishing Corporation.

PRINTED IN THE UNITED STATES OF AMERICA

10 9 8 7 6 5 4 3 2 1

chapter
~1~

MISS EMILY SEETON was halfway up the splendid central staircase at the Royal Academy of Arts in Piccadilly early in the afternoon of a fine July day in 1972 when it was embarrassingly drawn to her attention that she had quite forgotten to deposit her umbrella at the cloakroom. This was understandable, since all manner of thoughts loosely connected with chess had been jostling each other in her mind during the twenty-minute walk from Charing Cross. This wasn't because she knew or cared much about the subject, but because the Reverend Arthur Treeves, the vicar of Plummergen in Kent, was a keen follower of the game and had got it into his head that she was something of an expert.

Quite how this had come about Miss Seeton was at a loss to understand, but the fact was that ever since Bobby Fischer had arrived in Reykjavik at the beginning of the month to challenge Boris Spassky, the vicar had seized every opportunity to solicit her opinions on the eccentric American's strengths and weaknesses and his prospects of success. He had indeed raised the subject again that very morning on the way to Brettenden, where he was to attend a meeting called by the Rural Dean. Miss Seeton gave him the chance to do so when she momentarily stopped thanking him for his kindness in giving her a lift to the station in his trusty Morris Minor, in order to admire a fine display of lobelia in the front garden of a cottage they were passing.

"Yes, yes. It vividly exemplifies the words of the well-loved hymn." Somewhat to Miss Seeton's surprise, Mr. Treeves began to sing, in a throaty but professionally forceful tenor. " 'He paints the wayside flower, He lights the evening star . . . ' " She was about to join in when he stopped and coughed in an embarrassed way. "The summer, I gather, is very brief indeed in Iceland, so Spassky and Fischer are hardly likely to see lobelia flourishing there. No doubt it comes as no surprise to you that Spassky won the first two games, Miss Seeton."

"Well, to be quite frank, Mr. Treeves, I must confess that—"

"Of course, of course. For my own part, I had rather hoped that . . . but then I am a complete duffer at the game myself, so who am I to challenge your opinion? It is just as well that I play only very occasionally, against old Mr. Meredith when I go to see him at the Eventide Home and Matron draws me aside to whisper that it happens to be one of his better days." The vicar sighed. "Alas, even then he tends to confuse the moves with those used in draughts, and one hesitates to . . ."

Thus it was that when Miss Seeton reached London and emerged from the terminus, almost the first thing that caught her eye was a boldly lettered poster announcing an early edition of the *Evening Standard*. It bore just the two words SPASSKY RESIGNS, and puzzled her enough to make her buy a newspaper, a thing she had not done for years. She stood beside the news vendor's stand and studied the brief report under the banner headline on the front page. Yes, it was the same Spassky, the Russian gentleman Mr. Treeves had been mentioning so often during the past few weeks, but it appeared that he hadn't resigned *from* anything: merely that he had conceded victory to Mr. Fischer in their current game. Oh, *good!* How happy the vicar would be!

After a short debate with herself Miss Seeton decided against keeping the newspaper to take back with her to Plummergen as a present for Mr. Treeves. It was too big to go in her bag, some of the ink had already come off on her fingers, and Mr. Treeves would undoubtedly hear the good news on the wireless during the course of the day. She therefore deposited the paper in a nearby litter bin and set off by way of the church of St. Martin-in-the-Fields and the National Gallery.

The latter, with the National Portrait Gallery tucked away behind it, might ordinarily have diverted Miss Seeton from her original plan to proceed directly to Burlington House to visit the Royal Academy's annual Summer Exhibition. However, she was so lost in thoughts prompted by the newspaper report that she had wandered along the north side of Trafalgar Square and turned into the Haymarket before she had even finished wondering why it was almost always chess, music, and mathematics that produced infant prodigies.

At least, that was the conventional wisdom, one seemed to remember. In spite of the fact that in all honesty, one would be hard put to it to name a celebrated infant mathematician. Or indeed any mathematician, unless you counted Albert Einstein, who as it happened was said also to have played the violin, but not very well. Good gracious, Piccadilly Circus already? Now the important thing was to be very careful about crossing the roads, until one reached Swan & Edgar's. After that it was plain sailing.

Had this Mr. Fischer, one wondered, been an infant prodigy? Like Mozart? Or Yehudi Menuhin? Mr. Treeves would probably know. From what he had said in the course of earlier conversations, he was not altogether a well-adjusted or happy man. Mr. Fischer, that is, not Mr. Menuhin, of course. Nor Mr. Treeves, even if he was something of a worrier. Perhaps all really outstanding chess players were, well, a little odd. It was, after all, difficult to understand why these two gentlemen should have decided to meet in Iceland, not the first country that sprang to mind as the ideal place to spend several weeks playing chess. Iceland's geysers were celebrated, of course, and—oh, my goodness, I'm here already and—"You can't bring *that* up here, madame!"

Miss Seeton treasured her splendid, indeed famous umbrella. The *Daily Negative*'s star reporter Amelita Forby sometimes said she would have liked to claim copyright in the phrase "Battling Brolly," which appeared at frequent intervals in her pieces and, depending on the context, denoted both the umbrella and its owner. In fact Mel was secretly proud that it had passed into general currency in the tabloid press. The gift of Chief Superintendent Delphick of Scotland Yard, the umbrella had been Miss Seeton's companion, protector, and usually accidental weapon in many an adventure.

Nevertheless, as an inveterate visitor to museums and art galleries, Miss Seeton was well aware of the universal and strict rule that such things must be left at the entrance to institutions of that kind, in the cloakroom invariably provided. She fully approved, and was both flustered and filled with a sense of guilt when the uniformed attendant at the top of the staircase began to descend towards her, pointing accusingly at the umbrella tucked comfortably under her arm. No longer young, he had a florid complexion, a large moustache, and an air of authority.

"Oh, dear, I am so very sorry," she quavered, even in her discomfiture thinking that the attendant looked quite remarkably like Lord Kitchener in the renowned First World War recruiting poster with its memorable exhortation YOUR

COUNTRY NEEDS YOU! Especially pointing like that. "I will take it to the cloakroom at once."

She spun round, unfortunately without looking behind her, and the ferrule of the umbrella caught in the waistcoat of a tall, distinguished-looking, elderly gentleman who was at that moment poised on one foot, the other being in midair as he mounted from one step to the next. Knocked off balance, he sprawled sideways and downwards, bounced off the large bosom of a lady so generously endowed that she absorbed the impact without herself being put off course, and ended up draped against the ornate wrought ironwork of the balustrade several steps farther down, clutching at the highly polished wooden handrail.

Miss Seeton looked down at him in horror. It was quite bad enough to have caused such an accident through her carelessness and clumsiness. It was a hundred times worse to recognise her victim as Sir Wormelow Tump, the Custodian of the Queen's Collection of Objets de Vertu.

"Another cucumber sandwich, Miss Seeton? Or one of these petits fours, perhaps?" Tump enquired politely a couple of hours later. "They're awfully good here, you know."

Miss Seeton shook her head, a regretful smile on her face. "Thank you, but I couldn't possibly manage any more. You are so very kind, particularly in view of my unpardonable—"

"Tush and taradiddle, dear lady! A dramatic reunion, I grant you, but no harm done. And after all, it gave me the pleasure of going round the exhibition in your company. You are no mean critic, if I may say so." A muscle twitched at the corner of his mouth.

From the moment that he had recognised Miss Seeton and realised at once that there was not the slightest point in making a fuss about the indignity to which she had unwittingly subjected him, Sir Wormelow had been having a fine time. No matter that he had hardly been able to get a word in edgeways. Miss Seeton's unerring eye for quality was as impressive as her comments were idiosyncratic but unfailingly enlightening. Yet she brimmed over with simple joy in art, and found something positive to say about everything that caught her eye, even daubs so amateurish that the selection committee should never have given them the nod.

"You flatter me, Sir Wormelow." While walking through the lofty galleries at Burlington House with so much to look at, it had been possible, well, not exactly to forget, but to cope with the fact that he was such an eminent person, and to chatter to him quite freely. Now, tête-à-tête with him in the opulent surroundings of the tea lounge at the Ritz Hotel, the full, appalling recollection of what she had done to him suddenly swamped her consciousness, and Miss Seeton looked around, simply to avoid his gaze. Fortune favoured her by providing the perfect distraction.

"Oh, look! Over there. Isn't that Mr. Szabo just sitting down?"

Tump peered over the top of his gold-rimmed half glasses in the direction indicated. "Good Lord, so it is! Bless my soul, this is turning into a real reunion. Why don't I ask him to join us?" Without waiting for a reply he stood up and made his way, napkin in hand, to where the dapper dealer in rare antiques and objets d'art was lowering himself into a gilt chair held for him by a deferential waiter. Two minutes later the waiter was laying a third place at their own table while Ferencz Szabo bent low over the back of Miss Seeton's hand and kissed the air half an inch above its surface.

"*Enchanté, chère madame!*" he exclaimed, straightening up. "Eet eese soch a plaisure . . ."

"Come off it, Frank," Tump said. "We're all old friends here."

"So we are, Wonky, so we are. Sorry, Miss Seeton,"

Szabo said in a perfectly ordinary voice without a trace of foreign accent. He sat down. "Lovely to see you again. I know all the best people have tea at the Ritz, but what brings you all the way from Plummergen?"

"The Royal Academy summer exhibition." Miss Seeton gazed earnestly into his eyes, now even more determined to avoid Tump's. "And I, er, ran into Sir Wormelow on the way in—"

"Actually, she jolly nearly—" Tump stopped abruptly and cleared his throat. "I mean, we jolly nearly missed each other." Greatly relieved, Miss Seeton glanced at him gratefully. "And now you come breezing in, Frank. Quite takes me back to that extraordinary day at Rytham Hall."

The waiter returned with further supplies of tea, miniature sandwiches, and exquisite little cakes, and Miss Seeton took advantage of the resulting bustle to take a good look at the newcomer and wonder whether she ought to continue to address him as Mr. Szabo, or as Mr. Taylor. She knew he had a justifiable claim to both names. Legally he was Frank Taylor, for many years a naturalised Briton, but he had been born Ferencz Szabo in the Hungarian city of Debrecen, and it was as Szabo that he traded, in his exclusive gallery in Bond Street, five minutes' walk away from where they were sitting. It was a couple of years since she had last seen him, and though he was as beautifully turned out as he had been then, he didn't look altogether well. Not that one could possibly mention it, of course.

"Are you quite well, Mr., er?" she heard herself asking not two seconds later. "Do forgive my, that is . . ."

Szabo cast a surprised look at her. "Goodness, do I look that bad? Or are you telepathic? I'm all right, thanks, but as a matter of fact I have this minute come from Harley Street. My doctor gave me such a wigging that it left me in urgent need of tea and—"

"Not sympathy, I hope, old boy?"

"Oh, *dear*, I do hope . . ."

"No, no. Nothing to worry about, I assure you." Miss Seeton and Wormelow Tump had given voice to their concern simultaneously and Szabo looked from one to the other of them, touched. "I have been rather under the weather lately, but I think I've just been overdoing things a bit, that's all. Nothing fundamentally amiss, the medic says. The reason he charged a lot of money to bully me is that he wants me to take a holiday, and I told him it's out of the question. A cruise, in the sunshine, he said. I ask you, how can I possibly just drop everything and go off on a cruise? Quite apart from the fact that I can't swim and I'm terrified of water." He scrutinised the plate of iced cakes rather sternly and selected one that perfectly matched his salmon pink tie.

"Depends on the cruise, I'd say." There was a mysterious little smile on Tump's aristocratic face. "Why not book yourself on a Heron Halcyon Holiday? They do provide lifeboats, you know."

"Halcyon Holidays? What an extraordinary coincidence! Just the other day Lady Colveden told me that she and Sir George are going on one of their cruises next month. To celebrate their twenty-fifth wedding anniversary."

"I know."

"I was confused, because halcyon *days* are in the winter, aren't they, but it seems that—did you say you *know*, Sir Wormelow?"

"Yes. A ten-day cruise on the liner *Eurydice*, stopping here and there among the Greek islands to visit various historic sites and antiquities. *Aegean Idyll*, this particular holiday's called, in spite of the fact that it begins in Venice. Actually, I was the one who suggested it to George Colveden. He wanted to surprise his wife."

"Surprise her? She must have been utterly astounded!" Szabo turned to Miss Seeton, a distinct sparkle now in his eyes. "I ought to explain. Since that business with the Lalique jewelry, Wormelow and I have kept in touch with George Colveden. His idea, originally, but I must admit we all—not forgetting Cedric Benbow, of course—we all enjoy getting together now and then for dinner at his club. Our last reunion was getting on for six months ago, which is why all this is news to me. George is a marvellous old boy, but hardly one to come up spontaneously with the idea of going to look at a lot of old ruins, wouldn't you agree?"

"Oh, but it sounds wonderful," Miss Seeton said, trying hard to keep the wistfulness out of her voice. "I'm so happy for Lady Colveden. But what made you think of it, Sir Wormelow?"

"Well, there are always three or four guest lecturers on board these Heron cruises, you see. So-called experts—"

"He's only saying 'so-called' because he's one himself, Miss Seeton. They're genuine experts, all right. Top people in their fields. I know about Heron Holiday cruises, and they really are rather special. It's just that I can't somehow see George Colveden fitting in altogether happily with a lot of, well, fairly dedicated seekers after culture."

"You're being jolly hard on the people who sign up, Frank. Making 'em sound like a lot of bores. Whereas, dash it all, you meet some thoroughly nice people on board the *Eurydice*. I wouldn't suggest it otherwise. I mean it, you know. Why don't you come too? Follow doctor's orders *and* brush up your professional patter at the same time?"

Szabo shook his head. "Not me. If and when I do take a holiday it won't be of the busman's variety. And it won't be afloat."

An expression of low cunning crept into Wormelow Tump's face. "Forgot to mention the other lecturers they've invited. The bishop—they always seem to have one—is a chap I'd never heard of before I saw the brochure, name of Ashley Bowdler. Bishop of Bromwich. Used to lecture in classics at Cambridge. Then there's Dr. Blodwen Griffiths, the coin expert, and, um, Adrian Witley.''

"Witley?" Szabo's face reddened with anger, and Miss Seeton felt quite anxious about him until, with what looked like a considerable effort of will, he recovered most of his customary debonair poise. "My dear Wonky, you can't seriously suppose that I would contemplate spending ten days on board a ship in the company of that ghastly man? No. Come what may, I'm afraid that not even the prospect of George Colveden's company—and yours, needless to say—could induce me to sign up for that particular Aegean Idyll.''

chapter

-2-

"Has he really? By Jove, that's good news! Hang on a jiffy while I tell Meg . . . oh, I can't. Just remembered, she's gone to Brettenden to get her hair done or something. She'll be delighted when she hears. Met him in the Ritz, did you? With Miss Seeton? Good Lord, d'you mean to say Frank Taylor's started squiring Miss Seeton about? Wonders will never cease."

"No, no, you've got the wrong end of the stick, George . . ." Major-General (retired) Sir George Colveden, Bt, DSO, JP, settled back in his battered old leather armchair and listened obediently while Tump again explained the circumstances that had led to his encounter with Miss Seeton, and their subsequent conversation over tea with Ferencz Szabo. Meantime he absentmindedly reached down and fondled the head of the dog that had followed him into the library at Rytham Hall when he went to answer the telephone, and was now slumped at his feet.

". . . and he told us his doctor had been nagging him to get away for a break. He was looking a bit seedy as a matter of fact. Said he'd been overworking, but I fancy I know what's really the matter with him."

"Something the matter with Frank, you say?"

"Not physically. It's just that he's involved in a complicated legal row that might develop into a libel action, and it's getting him down. I won't bore you with the details, but the other party's a fellow called Adrian Witley. He's a professor of archaeology, but you might have seen him on the television.''

"Witley . . . Witley. Rings a bell, yes. Yes, of course. He's the obnoxious chap with the curly hair. On that idiotic *Ask Me Another* show. Extraordinary thing, Wonky, but Meg's a bit of a fan of his. Won't hear a word against him. Been upsetting Frank, has he? Can't have that.''

"Strictly between you and me, George, this business promises to turn into a first-class scandal. A few months ago a bust of Homer came up for auction in a sale of antiquities at Sotheby's. Frank had reason to think it was a fake, and said as much. Even though it had been authenticated by Adrian Witley. In spite of the nonsense he gets up to on television, Witley is a recognised authority. Whereas, while Frank has become extremely knowledgeable over the years, he's never pretended to be a scholar. So what it comes down to is that Witley's putting it about that Frank's nothing but a pushy ignoramus, while Frank for his part has certainly implied—to me at least and probably to others—that Witley is prepared to put his seal of approval on fakes if the money's right.''

"Well, judging by what I've seen of the blighter smirking and showing off on television, *my* money's on good old Frank. Anyway, I'm tickled pink to think he's going to be on this cruise.''

"When I first suggested it he wouldn't hear of it. Said he can't swim and has been terrified of water since childhood. Even the thought of lifeboat drill upsets him. Then I told him that as it happens, Adrian Witley's one of the guest lecturers.''

"Really? Good heavens, I wonder if Meg knows?''

"She ought to. All our names are in the brochure.''

"Brochure? What brochure? Oh, you mean all that bumph the travel agent sent. Haven't bothered my head with it, to tell you the truth, but Meg reads it every morning over breakfast. Must have learned it off by heart by now. Fancy her not mentioning this Witley chap! Of course, I suppose she might have done, when I wasn't listening. Does happen now and then. I say, Wonky?"

"Yes?"

"Don't quite follow you, old man. If Frank can't stand Witley's guts, why does he want to go on a cruise with him?"

"He didn't, at first. In fact, his initial reaction when I mentioned Witley's name was to say that nothing would induce him to join us. But by the following morning he'd changed his mind, as I'd suspected he would. You see, he's convinced that Witley's a crook in league with one or two shady dealers, but needs to be able to prove it if it does come to a full-blown libel action. And after thinking about it, Frank reckons that by keeping Witley under observation at close quarters for over a week he might be able to catch him out."

"Doing what?"

"My word, George, you've taken hold of this like a terrier, haven't you? Didn't think you'd be so interested. Well, you've got to bear in mind that among the passengers on the cruise there'll be a good many wealthy people, and a good many connoisseurs and serious collectors. During the various excursion visits on shore they won't only be looking at ruins and going round museums. They'll make a beeline for up-market antique shops. Then again, dealers—who know all about the sort of people who go on Heron Halcyon Holidays—will be hanging around them practically everywhere they go. Frank will be very interested to see the sort of company Witley keeps in his free time. So shall I, come to that."

"You don't say! I never dreamt we could look forward to such goings-on."

"You wish to see me, sir?"

"Morning, Delphick. Yes. Sorry to drag you away from your desk. Have a seat." The assistant commissioner (Crime) at New Scotland Yard pushed his own chair back a few inches and surveyed his visitor. Chief Superintendent Delphick settled himself comfortably and smiled amiably back.

"Have much contact with the art fraud investigation unit, do you? In the normal run of things, I mean."

"A certain amount, sir. You may recall that Inspector Madison reports to me."

A look of deep suspicion on his face, Sir Hubert Everleigh swung his swivel chair round and peered for several seconds at the framed organisation chart hanging on the wall beside him. Then he turned back to face Delphick again, his expression now one of slight embarrassment. "You're quite right, so he does. It says so there in black and white, on my chart."

"'A prudent man concealeth knowledge,'" Delphick murmured.

"What was that?"

"Book of Proverbs, sir. Chapter twelve, if my memory serves."

"Know what the trouble with you is, Oracle? It's that I never know whether you intend to be cheeky, or whether it simply comes out that way."

"No, sir, I suppose you don't."

"But spare me any more quotations for the time being, will you?"

"As you wish, sir."

"Right. Yes. I do wish. Let me begin again. Has In-

spector Madison by any chance mentioned a dispute about
a bust of Homer to you?''

"No, sir, he hasn't.''

"Thank heavens for that. I don't think I could have stood
it if you already knew. Well, let me tell you something for
once.'' The assistant commissioner consulted the paper
lying on his blotter. From where he was sitting Delphick
could see only that it had a few notes on it scribbled in
Everleigh's own hand.

"This bust of Homer came up for sale at Sotheby's a few
weeks ago, I gather. At least, it was supposed to. In the
catalogue and so forth. But then its authenticity was put in
question. By the owner of the Szabo Gallery in Bond
Street.''

"Ferencz Szabo!''

"The same. Also known as Frank Taylor. The man who
stopped that jewel thief in his tracks by shouting at him in
the voice of a regimental sergeant major. Can't remember,
were you among those present, Delphick?''

"Alas, no.''

"Too bad. Must have been a memorable show. Anyway,
this Szabo or Taylor seems to have stuck his neck out rather,
because the bust in question had been declared kosher by
an eminent expert, who took grave offence. Not only that,
he counter-claimed that Szabo's nothing but a jumped-up
rag and bone man who wouldn't know a bust of Homer
from one of Mae West.'' The AC permitted himself a smile.
"Those are the colourful terms in which your old friend Sir
George Colveden put it when he buttonholed the chief constable of Kent yesterday at his local golf club.''

"Colveden? Szabo? Why should he—oh, of course. I
recall Sergeant Ranger telling me that Colveden was very
impressed by Szabo's performance in the fracas at Rytham
Hall.''

"He was indeed, and keeps in touch with him. Also

Wormelow Tump and the photographer chap, Benbow.
They dine together at Colveden's club every so often, but
that's beside the point. Which is, that the controversial bust
has been temporarily withdrawn, and there's some talk of
a libel action. I expect Madison can fill you in.''

"Very possibly, sir, but it's hardly a police matter,
surely?''

"Obviously not, but you don't imagine a little thing like
that bothers George Colveden, do you?''

"Ah. I see what you mean. What does he want?''

"He wants us to send Miss Seeton on a cruise round the
Greek islands.''

"Miss Seeton? What on earth for?''

"If you'd shut up for two minutes instead of bombarding
me with questions, I might have a chance to explain, confound it.''

"Sorry, sir. I'm all ears.''

"All right, then, new readers begin here. Colveden's
taking his wife on this cruise, to celebrate their twenty-fifth
wedding anniversary. It's one of these highbrow cultural
affairs, where they cart a bunch of high-priced experts along
to lecture at the passengers. Hardly Colveden's cup of tea,
one would have thought, but there you are. Now one of the
lecturers happens to be Wormelow Tump, and another this
fellow that Szabo's tangling with. Professor Adrian Witley
. . . wait a minute, I haven't finished yet.''

Everleigh consulted his notes briefly, and then went on.
"You're quite right, though, it is Witley, the television
personality. I can't stand the chap personally. Can't for the
life of me understand why my wife looks like a lovesick
schoolgirl whenever she watches his show, but that's by the
way, I suppose. Back to business. According to Colveden,
Szabo's decided to go along on this cruise too, because he
thinks this Homer bust affair's just the tip of the iceberg.
He reckons Witley's involved in some crooked scheme to

slip fake antiquities onto the market, and hopes to be able to catch him in the company of some unsavoury associates. There, I think I've covered everything. Your turn now."

"Thank you. I'm afraid I do have some more questions."

"Fire away," Sir Hubert said, all geniality again.

"I'm assuming that the Kent chief constable dumped all this in the commissioner's lap——"

"Somewhat disrespectful way of putting it, but yes, he did. And the commissioner dumped it in mine half an hour ago, and now I'm dumping it in yours."

"The thing is, who's going to pay, sir? For Miss Seeton to sail around the Greek islands sketching anybody she spots whispering in Professor Witley's ear or slipping him bundles of used banknotes? That's presumably what George Colveden has in mind."

"Bang on. But we don't have to pay her. She's on our payroll anyway."

"All she gets from us is a very modest annual retainer. Plus expenses. But in providing for payment of Miss Seeton's expenses, we didn't have in mind lashing out on a single cabin on a cruise liner for ten days, just because a friend of the chief constable of Kent has a bee in his bonnet. My department's on a very tight budget, sir. If I'm right, this is a Heron Halcyon Holiday we're talking about, and they don't come cheap. It seems to me that unless there's a clear CID interest in finding out more about Professor Witley's activities, we ought to tell George Colveden that if he wants Miss S along on this cruise, he should invite and pay for her as his personal guest."

That's one in the eye for old Sir Heavily, Delphick thought to himself as he watched his superior's eyebrows shoot up. The old boy network's all very fine—where should we be without it?—but it really was pretty cool for George Colveden to more or less snap his fingers and give his instructions just because one of his golfing cronies happens to be an important copper.

Not that it was altogether a bad idea. The thought of the Colvedens, Ferencz Szabo, and Wormelow Tump all literally in the same boat, or ship rather, had a certain baroque charm. That Adrian Witley was also to be aboard added piquancy. According to Mrs. Delphick, clearly a less susceptible viewer than Lady Everleigh, Witley obviously thought he was God's gift to women. Certainly he came across on the *Ask Me Another* celebrity quiz show as a pretty oily sort of character. Szabo on the other hand was a very shrewd fellow who deserved to be taken seriously if he thought Witley was up to no good. Most important of all was the fact that Miss S would almost certainly love the chance to cruise round the Greek islands, especially in the company of several good friends. It would be a discreet way of rewarding her for her unique past services, and go some way to make amends for the miserable pittance they paid her . . .

". . . a couple of thousand, perhaps. Are you listening to me, Delphick?"

"Indeed I am, sir. As always. Er, you were saying?"

"I was saying we might be able to squeeze another couple of thousand out of the contingency account to add to your CID slush fund in the current financial year."

"Three, sir."

"*Three?* For heaven's sake, it's only going to cost five or six hundred at most!"

"Three thousand, sir. Recurrent, in real terms of course, in subsequent financial years. If that could be arranged I'd consider it entirely proper for Miss Seeton to be given this assignment."

"Delphick, you are an unprincipled, unprintable, triple asterisk *scoundrel*!"

"Yes, sir. Thank you, sir. I'll check that it is a Heron

Halcyon Holiday, and that Miss Seeton's free to accept. I expect she'll jump at it. Then we'll book her a nice comfortable cabin. After you've signed the authorisation for the transfer of funds, of course."

"Go away, Delphick. Before I'm tempted to commit a serious crime myself."

"Certainly, sir. We endeavour to give satisfaction."

Miss Emily Seeton put the telephone down and sank back into her easy chair in the pleasant little living room at Sweetbriars, her retirement home in the village of Plummergen. Martha Bloomer had recently washed the chintz loose covers and hung them out to dry in the garden, and the smell of sunshine clung about the chair. Miss Seeton had inherited the cottage from her late godmother while still teaching art at a girls' school in the North London suburb of Highgate— a pleasant district but one she had happily abandoned when her teaching days were over. Now she thought of Plummergen as home, and lived there for the most part in great contentment.

At that moment, however, she felt weak with excitement, hardly able to comprehend her good fortune. The Greek islands! Lands of gods and heroes! From the moment dear Lady Colveden had mentioned her forthcoming cruise with Sir George one had tried so hard not to succumb to demeaning feelings of envy, but rather to feel happy for them. By borrowing that fascinating book from the Brettenden public library, for instance.

With its evocative chapter headings: "Corfu, Paxos, Antipaxos;" "Lemnos, Thasos, and Samothrace." The very names were invocations, even if Paxos did make one think of the brand of stuffing mix that Mr. Stillwell sold in his shop. And it was on Paxos, according to the book, that Mr. Gladstone had bowed his head to receive the blessing of its Orthodox bishop, who hesitated so long that Mr. Gladstone concluded he must be ineligible and suddenly raised it again, dealing the dignitary a smart blow on the chin. But it probably hadn't hurt very much, because the bishop would have been luxuriantly bearded, no doubt.

And thinking of Paxo brand stuffing, how interesting that Mr. Stillwell also sold Cos lettuces. In season, of course. One did so hope it wouldn't be a disappointment. To Lady Colveden, that is. For whom the cruise had originally been intended to have romantic associations. The news that one had been invited to go too, and—so extraordinarily generous of him—at Sir George's suggestion.

Perhaps it had already saddened Lady Colveden to learn that Sir Wormelow Tump as a distinguished guest lecturer was to be a fellow passenger. She must have realised at once that he hadn't thought it up himself as an imaginative anniversary present after all. Sir George, that is. But that his friend Sir Wormelow must have suggested the idea. Not that Lady Colveden gave the impression of expecting flights of fancy of Sir George, but even so . . .

And now, according to Mr. Delphick, Mr. Szabo had decided to join the party as well! Oh, dear, it began to seem that for Lady Colveden the cruise would not inspire tender thoughts of her wedding twenty-five years earlier, but remind her of that unfortunate business of the attempted theft of the Lalique jewelry from her house.

Obviously there was no possibility of any untoward incidents this time. Mr. Delphick had explained that. It was because it had been decided at Scotland Yard to give one a "merit award," which for some technical reason couldn't take the form of cash. It was for the Identikit drawings one had done from time to time, presumably. The award, that is. So Mr. Delphick had consulted one or two of her acquaintances, including Sir George. And as a result, quite soon, they would be real places one could treasure in one's memory, not only names, however magical! Seriphos, Siphnos and Mikos; Mykonos and Delos; Lesbos—

Miss Seeton blushed slightly.

chapter
~3~

"THERE HE IS, over there," Adrian Witley said in Italian, indicating from his vantage point on the balcony of the Doge's Palace a little knot of people standing at the foot of one of the impressive columns at the seaward end of the Piazza San Marco: the one that bore the winged lion statue, symbol of the city of Venice. "Blast him," he added in English, rather unnecessarily, since his companion—who was fluent in that language and several others—already knew his views on the subject of Ferencz Szabo.

"Where? Oh, yes, I see him now." Carlo Crivelli nodded, for he knew also what Szabo looked like. "Who are the people with him? Are they all going on board the *Eurydice* too?"

A bulky man in his late forties, with a slightly squashed-looking nose and dark, vaguely sorrowful eyes, Crivelli might have been taken by a passing stranger at first glance for anything from a retired pugilist to a family doctor. A more observant person would have noted the expensive cloth and impeccable cut of his suit and decided that, if a medical man at all, he was probably a cosmetic surgeon with a fashionable clientele, who charged the earth for his services.

"Yes, they are. I'm sure about most of them, anyway. I called at the Heron Holidays office before I left London and managed to persuade them to let me have a look at the passenger list. And the names of people they'd booked to fly from London to Milan and on to here. The tall one's Wormelow Tump. I thought you knew him.''

"I know who he is, naturally. I've never met him, though.''

"The red-faced man with the moustache must be Sir George Colveden, with his wife. Friends of Tump's, I believe. I don't know who the elderly lady with the umbrella is. Oh, she's wandering off on her own anyway. Probably no connection.''

"They arrived yesterday, did they?''

"That was the arrangement. So they'll have had the best part of today for sightseeing before we all go on board the ship between four-thirty and five-thirty.'' Witley once more reverted to English. "*Damn* the man! 'Frank Taylor' indeed! Greasy little foreigner.'' Belatedly he noticed the bleakly hostile look that Crivelli was directing at him. "No offence, Charles,'' he added hastily, but the Italian was not to be mollified that easily.

"My name is *Carlo*,'' he said, his voice silky but charged with distaste. "I permit a few of my English-speaking *friends* to address me as Charles. But since to you I am obviously nothing but a 'greasy foreigner,' or 'Wop' perhaps, I would prefer you to revert to 'Signor Crivelli.' ''

"For heaven's sake, man, it was a stupid remark and I apologise, but there's no need to fly off the handle! I haven't called you Signor Crivelli for at least two years, and we've been doing good business with each other since then. Not to mention in the three days since I arrived here. And you have just as much reason to detest Szabo as I do.''

Crivelli stared at the Englishman for a long moment, and then almost imperceptibly shrugged. "Very well. I accept your apology. Now listen to me. Since you got here I have behaved as if there is nothing much amiss, but you must have wondered why I have booked myself on this cruise of yours. It's now time for some plain speaking. This silly television nonsense has gone to your head, Adrian. You've become vain and overconfident, and in our business that could lead to disaster. People may stop you in the street and ask for your autograph in England, but you don't cut any ice here, you know. Bear this in mind. In the past you have had your uses for a number of us, and we've paid you well for your services. Now you're becoming an embarrassment. Your discretion is in question.''

''You know I'm discreet, Charles.'' Witley sounded a little uncertain.

''My associates and I aren't so sure. We'd like to know how Szabo came to have doubts about the Homer bust in the first place. And how you propose to deal with him.''

''The best libel lawyer in London has been retained—''

''Szabo is not poor, nor is he a fool. He has access to good lawyers as well. You know very well you can't afford to let this business get to the point of a court action. Nor can my associates. No, you'll have to do better than that, Professor Witley.'' Witley looked at him in consternation. It wasn't distaste he heard in Crivelli's voice now, but naked menace.

''I—I don't understand. And what's all this 'Professor Witley' stuff?''

''In a few hours we shall both be on board the *Eurydice*. When we meet, we shall not know each other, except by repute. Crivelli will of course have heard of the eminent British scholar, and Witley will know of the existence of the wealthy Italian collector. Does that make sense to you, Professor Witley?''

''Oh, I see. Yes, it does, er, Signor Crivelli.''

''Good. Now, as to the other matter, don't be obtuse. We have decided that Szabo must be eliminated; something that should have been obvious to you for weeks. If you are to retain your credibility with us, you are the one who must dispose of him, and you must do it before the end of the cruise. I am joining the cruise in order to make sure you do.''

"I say, anybody know where Miss Seeton's got to?"

"Haven't a clue. I noticed her drifting off while we were deciding where to go for lunch," Szabo said. "Don't worry about her, George. She's probably decided to skip food and go and have a look at those Carpaccios she's keen to see."

"But dash it all, she doesn't speak the lingo, Frank. Might get lost, never find her way back."

"Don't be such an old fusspot, darling." Far from resenting the company of the two art experts her husband had so improbably taken to his bosom as cronies, Lady Colveden was delighted to think that he was now looking forward to the cruise as much as she was. As for Miss Seeton, well, she was always good value.

Exactly what dear old George thought he'd been up to in pulling strings to get her included in the party remained to be seen. He had been comically evasive when she taxed him on the subject, after Miss Seeton had telephoned her with some incoherent story about a Scotland Yard merit award made on George's recommendation. Never mind. Meg Colveden had, by taking her time over it, seen through far too many of her husband's appealingly incompetent attempts at duplicity to have the slightest doubt that all would become clear to her in due course.

Meantime it was fun to observe the childlike pleasure Miss Seeton had taken in everything so far. Her hurried preparations for the trip had involved a number of consultations about clothes, but since Meg Colveden seriously doubted if most of her advice actually registered with Miss Seeton, she had taken the precaution of repeating it privately to the unfailingly commonsensical Martha Bloomer. And

Mrs. Bloomer had duly succeeded in presenting a shyly smiling Miss Seeton and two only slightly bulging suitcases at the front gate of Sweetbriars when the Colvedens arrived in the hire car that was to take them all to Heathrow Airport for the flight to Venice via Milan.

"I don't know about fusspot," Sir George protested. "Single British lady wandering about abroad, and all that. You never know."

"Really, George! I hardly think Miss Seeton's in much danger of having her bottom pinched."

"And certainly not in the Scuola Dalmatia," Szabo pointed out with a smile.

"The where?"

"The museum where the Carpaccios are."

"What on earth have Dalmatians got to do with it? Not that I've anything against them as a breed, mind you. Very intelligent dogs."

"Not dogs, George. People. From Dalmatia. It was a sort of guild headquarters for them here in Venice. Meeting hall downstairs where the paintings are, chapel of St. George upstairs. Carpaccio was a Dalmatian. So was St. George, for that matter."

"You sure? I could have sworn he was English. My parents certainly thought so. That's why they named me after him."

Accustomed to Sir George's scatter-shot conversational style, Szabo pressed on imperturbably. "And we've already been to the harbour to have a look at the ship and dump our stuff at the luggage office, so Miss S knows where to go if she misses us. Tell you what, though, I wouldn't mind seeing those paintings myself, so I'll saunter over there and take her under my wing, if you like. Care to join me, Meg?"

Lady Colveden glanced towards her husband, just in time to catch him winking at Tump and nodding his head in a conspiratorial way. "Yes, I think I would. Would you mind, George?"

"Good Lord no! Splendid idea," he said heartily, adjusting his expression in haste. "I'll give it a miss myself, I think. Thought Wonky and I might have a drink and a bit of a chinwag before lunch. If that would suit you, old boy?"

"By all means." It was Tump's turn to catch Lady Colveden's eye, and the wink he bestowed on her was infinitely more subtle than the ones Colveden had been so strenuously aiming at him. "Off you go, the pair of you. If you don't turn up at the Madonna restaurant for lunch at about one, let's all rendezvous at the harbour at four, shall we?"

"Bravo, Wonky," Colveden said, having waved cheerily at his wife and her eminently trustworthy escort as they walked off. "Jolly impressive, the way you twigged I wanted to have a private word with you. I say, isn't that the television feller over there? Whitlow or whatever his name is? My word, those makeup people must know their job. Last time Meg insisted on watching that show of his he looked full of beans. Whereas, as you can see, in normal life he's like a dying duck in a thunderstorm, not that I've ever really understood that, the way I see it, if I were a dying duck I don't think I'd care much what the weather was doing, would you?"

Having waited patiently for his friend to run out of breath, Tump nodded. "It is Adrian Witley, yes. And you're right, he does look rather green about the gills. You don't suppose he's *following* Meg and Frank, do you?"

"Whatever for? Going on what you told me, I should have thought he's going to have a very nasty shock later on when he runs into old Frank lounging on board in a deck chair, what? Bound to, sooner or later. Can't see why he'd feel like seeking him out for the sake of it, though. No, pure coincidence, old boy, take my word for it. You know, I was going to suggest we might drop in at this Harry's Bar place they talk about. A chap I know told me once that the bullfighting feller used to go there all the time.''

"Ernest Hemingway."

"That's him. Fond of his drink, according to my friend. But look, it's beastly hot, and there's a sort of open-air pub place over there that looks all right. Suit you?"

The two men sat down at a vacant table, and Colveden ordered two beers, addressing the waiter very slowly. Then he looked at Tump rather sheepishly. "Just remembered you can speak the lingo."

"A little. But I imagine the waiter understands English perfectly well." The waiter in question was young and lissom, and had exchanged a meaningful look with Tump, who was already very much regretting not having made his acquaintance the previous day.

"Look, what I wanted to talk to you about is this whole business of keeping a friendly eye on Miss Seeton. Because take my word for it, she's going to be the key to this whole scheme . . ."

Blissfully unaware that she was the subject of discussion by Colveden and Tump, or that she was being sought in a desultory sort of way by Szabo and Lady Colveden, Miss Seeton was enjoying getting to know Dr. Dorcas Bookbinder. Dr. Bookbinder had come to her rescue and helped her to retrieve the contents of her handbag, which had somehow become inverted while she was negotiating the purchase of her ticket of admission to the Scuola Dalmatia.

During the hour that followed Dr. Bookbinder proved to be a most agreeable and well-informed companion. This was, Miss Seeton told herself, hardly to be wondered at, inasmuch as the American lady's doctorate was in the history of art, with special reference to the Venetian School. That she was well informed, that is. Agreeability did not necessarily go hand in hand with erudition, of course. Nevertheless Dr. Bookbinder, or Dorcas as she had been kind enough to insist on being called as soon as she discovered that they were to be fellow passengers during the forthcoming Aegean Idyll, was. Agreeable. Perhaps a trifle earnest, but that was no doubt due to a puritan upbringing in New England. How interesting it was that Old England, or Olde Englande, to be more precise, was associated with roast beef and merriment that sometimes verged upon the . . . well, indecorous, while New England conjured up quite contrasting images.

"Though in fact you would have fitted in perfectly, my dear!"

"Emily, you haven't been paying attention."

"Oh, dear, I'm afraid I haven't. You see, I was thinking that you don't look in the least bit like a puritan lady."

It was quite true. Dorcas Bookbinder was, as a matter of fact, thirty-six but looked younger. She wore only the merest trace of makeup, and had been frowning at the paintings through a formidable pair of glasses, but her skin was like satin, her hair silky-smooth, her eyes lustrous, and her lips soft and full. The light cotton dress she was wearing was entirely seemly, but hinted at a well-rounded body that Miss Seeton had at first sight decided Renoir would have loved to paint. Dr. Bookbinder's physical charms and her solemnity of manner were in combination altogether enchanting, and Miss Seeton was not in the least offended when, after they had introduced themselves to each other, the much younger woman forthwith addressed her as Emily, having clearly decided that she needed to be taken in hand.

Dorcas Bookbinder clearly knew her Carpaccios. They had lingered before the fresco called *The Triumph of St. George*, admired the strength of the saint's face, and gone back for a second look at the painting near the door that depicted him slaying the dragon. They winced together at the gory detail in the background of that one, and smiled at the gentle humour of another, in which the great painter showed several monks hastily making themselves scarce when St. Jerome turned up at their monastery accompanied by his tame lion.

Miss Seeton had previously seen only reproductions of these treasures, and was delighted to be shown the originals by an expert whose enthusiasm for them matched her own, but who knew so much more than she about the artist, and about the history of the small but beautifully proportioned building in which they were displayed.

"Oh, dear," she sighed when her private conducted tour was over and they were making their way out. "I do hope I shall have an opportunity to come back again one day. You made me see those paintings with new eyes, my dear. Thank you so much."

The Scuola Dalmatia is situated on a corner site, with a canal running along its side. As the two women were emerging from its entrance at the front, Szabo and Meg Colveden were approaching by way of the canal path. This was so narrow that Meg went first, with Szabo behind. Adrian Witley, still in more or less aimless pursuit, was slinking along behind, turning over wild and improbable ideas about how he might rid himself both of Szabo his enemy and Crivelli his tormentor.

For a brief, tantalising moment, fortune favoured him. A humpbacked bridge crosses the canal at the corner of the Scuola Dalmatia, and just as Meg Colveden turned to her left, saw Miss Seeton emerging from the entrance with her companion and greeted her with a glad cry, a party of a dozen or more gum-chewing teenage Italian schoolboys came jostling, reeling, pushing, and shoving their way over the bridge from the other side, generating a remarkable amount of noise and confusion.

Realising that his quarry was temporarily cut off from

the others, Witley ran up behind him and gave him a violent push that sent Szabo, arms flailing, face forwards into the malodorous waters of the canal. The schoolboys were much too involved in their own noisy horseplay to notice what was happening until Witley had slipped behind them and made his escape over the bridge.

chapter

~4~

"IT'S ALL VERY well for you, Wonky. It isn't your wife that's gone missing." Sir George looked at his watch for the umpteenth time. The hands stood at three forty-five, as they had done when he last looked at it ten seconds previously.

"I'm sure you needn't worry. We did say four o'clock, after all. The three of them are probably having a cup of tea somewhere. Be here in a jiffy, I should—there, what did I tell you? Here they come now..." Tump's voice trailed off into silence as he watched not three but four people approaching the gangway of the cruise liner *Eurydice* beside which the two men were standing.

Miss Seeton was making her way towards the ship in her usual sedate fashion, a little apart from the others. This was partly because she was employing her umbrella as a parasol, and also because in her free hand she was carrying a shapeless, sodden bundle. Lady Colveden and Dr. Bookbinder were on either side of the drooping form of Ferencz Szabo, each holding one of his arms and almost literally supporting him.

He was a pitiful sight. He wore shoes but no socks, and his legs were bare below the knees. His hair, normally a little masterpiece of the coiffeur's art, stood up in odd little spikes where it wasn't plastered to his skull, and his face was the face of a man who had recently undergone a traumatic experience.

"Good God!" Sir George exclaimed. "Why on earth is Frank dressed up in a bedsheet?"

"I can't say, George, but it might be a good idea for us to lend a hand, don't you think?"

Half an hour later Sir Wormelow Tump and Miss Seeton were standing at the rail beside the gangway watching other passengers boarding. "That's an elegant couple," he remarked as a lady in what she had every reason to consider her prime made her way up the gangway, followed by a good-looking man wearing a natty blazer and beautifully cut grey trousers. "They put me in mind of the two central figures in *The Embarkation to Cythera*. You know. Watteau."

"What ho!" the new arrival said, sounding pleasantly surprised to be greeted so affably. "Delighted to meet you."

Further confusion was avoided by the need for them to make way for other arriving passengers, and Tump and Miss Seeton withdrew a few yards before resuming their conversation. Knowing that Szabo had fallen into the canal, had been rescued and taken to the nearest bar where he had been given a restorative glass of grappa and Lady Colveden had negotiated the purchase of a tablecloth for him to wear in place of his ruined, evil-smelling clothes, was something.

Knowing that Szabo had been hastily escorted to his cabin and thence, after the morale-raising luxury of a long, hot shower, to the sick bay where he was currently being examined by the ship's doctor was reassuring. What Tump really wanted to know, however, was precisely how Szabo's misfortune had come to pass. He was not optimistic about his prospects of enlightenment by Miss Seeton, but thought it worth trying to find out what he could from her. Sooner

or later he could check what she said against what he was
sure would be a brisk, unvarnished account by Lady Colveden. Szabo himself would not want to be reminded of it.

"You say that a gang of schoolboys were involved, Miss
Seeton?"

"Oh, hardly *involved*, you know. Boys of that age can
be very boisterous, Sir Wormelow, as I expect you remember."

"Very good of you to put it like that, but it's a long time
since I was a schoolboy, boisterous or otherwise. Teenagers,
you said. A friend of mine has a good name for rowdy
groups of Italian lads. He calls them *slobberini*. Anyway,
d'you suppose one of them pushed Frank into the canal?
Deliberately, I mean?"

"Oh, I should be very unhappy to think such a thing. It
is much more likely to have been accidental. Oh, I have
just remembered something."

"You have?" Tump smiled at her encouragingly.

"Yes. The Watteau painting. It has been suggested that
the title is misleading, and that there is a certain sadness
about the scene. That the couples depicted are regretfully
leaving Cythera, where they have been happy. Not setting
out to go there."

"Feeling a weeny bit better now, are we?"

As it happened, Szabo was feeling a lot better as he
emerged from the sick bay, but far from being a hundred
per cent fit. He was therefore unprepared to be dazzled by
the hundred-watt smile being directed at him by the young
man apparently waiting for him outside. He closed his eyes
momentarily, shook his head a couple of times, and then
opened them again. It helped.

"Sorry," he said. "Didn't remember you for a moment.
You're the steward who showed me the way here, aren't
you?"

The steward pouted slightly, but then smiled forgivingly. "Marty Hussingtree at your service. I had hoped I'd made a bit of an impression, but there you go. Well, you'd had a horrid time, hadn't you, poor thing? Off we go, then, I'll show you the way back. I've made your cabin all nice again, but ooh, the *clothes*!" With the thumb and forefinger of his left hand, Hussingtree delicately pinched the tip of his nose, grimacing comically. "Talk about pong!"

Szabo did not want to be reminded of being fished out of the canal, of slopping and squelching miserably to the bar, of shivering and retching in the men's lavatory as he peeled off the stinking garments and wrapped himself in the tablecloth.

"Oh, lord, did somebody bring them here? Get rid of them for me, there's a good chap."

"Shame really, I looked at the labels. Wish I could afford such nice things—love that dressing gown, by the way—but very wise. I mean, it's not like the old saying, is it, you never know where they've been. 'Cos we *do* know where they've been, don't we?"

"Do we?" Szabo asked a little stiffly.

"Why of *course* we do, you tease! It's all over the ship. Such excitement!"

Szabo followed gloomily as the steward led the way, prattling happily. Oh, Lord, he thought, what a hell of a way to start a holiday. A ghastly experience, an expensive set of clothes totally ruined, everybody on the ship sniggering about him, and to crown it all, a gay cabin steward who obviously fancied his chances. Oh, well, with a bit of luck the young man'd catch Wonky Tump's eye, and that'd be one less thing to contend with, at least.

chapter
~5~

ALONE AT LAST and ensconced in what she decided was a perfectly delightful single cabin with its own porthole—no, one must remember to call it a scuttle, according to the charming steward—Miss Seeton had been in such a ferment of excitement that she decided that the only thing to be done to calm herself down was to run through a few of her yoga exercises. One thing led to another and she became oblivious to the passage of time. She was sitting cross-legged on the floor beside her bed with her eyes closed and exhaling forcibly through her nose when a tapping at the door disturbed her concentration.

More tapping, and then, "Emily? Are you ready, Emily?"

It took a second or two for Miss Seeton to remember where she was, but recognition of Dorcas Bookbinder's cultivated American accent with its overtones of slight censoriousness was then instantaneous, as was the sense of mingled guilt and embarrassment that swept over her.

"Oh, dear! One moment, please!" she called out, scrambling hurriedly to her feet and reaching for the dressing gown she had hung on the back of the door. Slipping into it, she unlatched the door and opened it to peep out. "How kind of you to remind me, er, Dorcas. I am so sorry to keep

you waiting, but I was in my, that is to say I am not yet
fully dressed. Do come in. Goodness, how pretty you look,
my dear!''

Dorcas Bookbinder didn't look altogether pleased at being
described as pretty, but entered the cabin anyway, and almost immediately spotted the well-worn copy of *Yoga and
Younger Every Day* lying face downward on the bed. She
picked it up, her face transformed by a delighted smile.
''Why, Emily! You're a yoga adept too! I might have
guessed it, you have that still centre to you, in spite of—''
she broke off, slightly pink at the thought of what she had
been on the point of saying.

Miss Seeton looked confused too, but in her case it was
out of natural humility. ''Dear me, no, still very much a
novice, coming as I did to it quite late in life . . . whereas
I'm sure you're, that is, how splendid to meet a fellow
enthusiast! In Plummergen one does sometimes feel a little,
not exactly ashamed, but, well, defensive, perhaps . . . oh,
dear, I'm making you late for the captain's reception, Dorcas, after you went to the trouble of explaining what time
I should get ready.''

''Don't give it a thought. After our little adventure earlier
I don't imagine the others are going to be surprised if we
show up at the welcome cocktail party a little late. And I
doubt if poor Mr. Szabo will bother to come at all. Listen,
Emily, why don't I come back for you in a few minutes,
after you've finished dressing?''

''So kind, but I really don't mind finding my own way.
It isn't such a very big boat, I mean ship, is it?''

''No, but I'll come back for you all the same. I'm going
to need your moral support at this party.''

As soon as Dorcas had left the cabin again, Miss Seeton
hastened to put on her best silk dress, wondering whatever the young woman could have meant by ''moral support.'' It was an unexpected thing for one so impressively

qualified, personable, and attractive to feel conscious of
needing.

"Ah, there you are!" As soon as he spotted Miss Seeton,
Sir George Colveden bustled over to her. "Well done, jolly
good. Come over and join the rest of us." He beamed at
Dorcas. "Evening, m'dear. I say, that's a pretty frock!"
Much to the amusement of his wife, Sir George had been
greatly smitten by the American woman from the moment
he met her, had thanked her profusely and with roguish
gallantry for going to the aid of Ferencz Szabo, and now
appeared to have cast himself in the role of elderly admirer.

"Good evening, Sir George. I see Mr. Szabo over there,
talking to Sir Wormelow Tump. I'm glad he feels well
enough to be with us," Dorcas said politely as Colveden
towed her and Miss Seeton across the lounge, full of well-
dressed people standing about with drinks in their hands,
sizing one another up. Few of them looked much under
forty, and for the most part they gave the impression of
being intelligent, sophisticated, and comfortably off.

"Old Frank? Rather, tough as an old boot, you know.
Ship's doctor looked him over and said he's as right as
ninepence, I'm told. What you'd expect of an old army
man. Mind you, those canals are pretty niffy, aren't they?
His clothes a total write-off, stank to high heaven, if you'll
forgive the expression. But he told me he kept his mouth
shut, and Miss Seeton here seems to have had him back on
terra firma before you could say Jack Robinson. You ever
wondered about that feller Robinson, Miss Seeton? Funny
thing to—"

"George, you're talking too much, darling." As they
approached, Lady Colveden cut in, and turned to the smiling
couple at her side. "Let me introduce Miss Emily Seeton,
a neighbour and dear friend of ours from Kent, and Dr.

Dorcas Bookbinder from America. This is Juliana Popjoy, and her friend Dickie Nash.''

During the confusion of hand-shaking, selection of drinks and canapes, and general reshuffle that ensued, Miss Seeton was able to form a better impression of her two new acquaintances than she had when she had seen them coming aboard, and Mr. Nash had been under the mistaken impression that Sir Wormelow had said "What ho!" to him. Definitely not a Watteau lady, she now decided. More like the subject of Rubens's *Le Chapeau de Paille*. No, wrong again, one had been too much influenced by the expanse of bosom Juliana Popjoy was displaying, and the fact that she was the sort of woman who seemed born to wear a broad-brimmed hat well decorated with feathers. No, the face was wider, the eyes serenely intelligent, the lips full but strong, and her whole poise that of a woman aware and proud of her sensuality. Of course! Juliana Popjoy was Goya's Doña Isabel de Porcel to the life.

Dickie Nash, by contrast, was a dandy, but weaker in character. An unkind person might see him as Philip IV of Spain as painted by Velazquez, perhaps, or Van Dyck's Charles I in hunting dress. Yet Mr. Nash was clearly a kindly and far from stupid man. One wasn't quite sure how those responsible set about choosing Fellows of King's College, Cambridge, but one could surely take it for granted that the candidates they considered were all persons of academic standing.

"... in Bath. Isn't that interesting, Miss Seeton?"

"I do beg your pardon, Lady Colveden, my attention was, er—"

"Juliana owns an antique shop in Bath."

"That's right. And Dickie's my sleeping partner," Juliana said in a matter-of-fact way; but her voice was as lush as her breasts, and there was a wicked look in her eye.

Dickie Nash hooked a thumb in the armhole of his brocade

waistcoat. "Absolutely. I get down to Bath as often as I can, but during term I'm pretty well stuck in Cambridge for eight whole weeks at a time. Such a bore."

"Eight whole weeks! Imagine! Doesn't your heart bleed for him?" Juliana demanded, amusement now written all over her face. "Does your university overwork you so shockingly, Dorcas? Dorcas? Are you feeling all right?" She reached out to put a supporting hand under the American's elbow and Dorcas momentarily clutched at it. She was very pale, but after a second or two seemed to recover, and even managed a tight little smile.

"I'm okay, thank you. I can't think what came over me."

Meg Colveden could. She had seen Adrian Witley enter the lounge. The Aegean Idyll cruise passengers were in general too civilised to react like starstruck teenagers to the sight of the television personality, but a slight hush nevertheless fell briefly over those in his vicinity before they resumed their conversations.

Not that Witley looked particularly glamorous. Male passengers had been advised that either black tie or lounge suit would be appropriate dress for the welcome party and the gala dinner to follow, and about half the men present—including Sir George Colveden, Ferencz Szabo, and Sir Wormelow Tump—were in fact wearing dinner jackets.

Witley was well enough turned out in a dark lounge suit, but inevitably lacked their impressive stylishness. Moreover, he seemed to be preoccupied to the point of distraction and barely acknowledged the friendly nods and smiles directed at him and his companion as they made their way to the far side of the lounge. There they joined the captain and the purser, who had moved across after earlier welcoming the majority of the passengers at the entrance, and were now in animated conversation with the two of them.

It was the woman with Witley who interested Meg Colveden and set her wondering whether it was the sight of her or of Witley himself that had so disconcerted Dorcas Book-binder. After a moment she decided that it was because they were together. Very much so, in the case of the woman at least. She was clinging to Witley's arm possessively and gazing at him in evident adoration, seemingly oblivious to the fact that he was virtually ignoring her.

Meg Colveden thought that not only ungentlemanly on Adrian Witley's part, but also rather foolish, for the woman was attractive in a willowy sort of way, with dark, softly curling hair and blue eyes of so dark a shade that they looked almost purple. She turned to Dickie Nash, who was looking in the same direction as herself. "Who's that over there with the captain, Dickie?" she asked him quietly.

"The smooth-looking character's an Italian collector, very rich, name of Carlo Crivelli. Juliana sold him a rather fine copy of an amphora once, only unfortunately she hadn't realised it was genuine. Antique dealers of all people have no right to feel sorry for themselves when that sort of thing happens, but she wasn't best pleased with Adrian Witley when Crivelli disposed of it a few months later for a small fortune."

"Why? What did Adrian Witley have to do with it?"

"Oh, as it happened he'd been in the shop a week or so earlier and rather poo-poohed the thing. Said it wasn't even a very good copy and that she'd overpriced it. A hundred to one the other chap's the Bishop of Bromwich. You can tell by his purple thingummy. I approve of the way they always bring a man of God along on these cruises, as well as a doctor. Makes one feel that if the worst were to happen one would be in expert hands, eased into the hereafter in the best possible taste."

"A very comforting thought, I agree. And that is Pro-fessor Witley, of course. I recognise him. Who's the woman with him?"

Somewhat to her surprise, Dickie Nash's hitherto amiable

expression was replaced by one of distaste. "Silly cow," he muttered, and then immediately apologised. "Sorry, Lady Colveden."

"Call me Meg, please."

"Yes, of course. Sorry to use such an unparliamentary expression, Meg. That is Dr. Blodwen Griffiths, university lecturer in ancient history and a leading expert on numismatics."

"She seems to be much attached to Professor Witley."

"Attached? I should think that if you were to peel her off him you'd hear a sucking noise."

"You obviously disapprove, Dickie."

Nash shrugged, his natural good humour reasserting itself. "Well, it's her business, of course, and as long as she's happy. No accounting for tastes, is there? All the same, some of us think quite a lot of her, and it's saddening to see her making such a fool of herself over a man like Witley."

Meg Colveden cleared her throat. "I must admit that he *is* rather attractive. On the television, at least. So I suppose he can hardly be blamed if women throw themselves at him and he . . ." A thought struck her. "Is he married, do you know?"

"No. Was at one time, I believe—"

"Excuse me." The voice was high and strained, and Meg Colveden was aghast when she turned her head to see Dorcas Bookbinder, her colour high, turn on her heel and sweep out of the room.

"Really, Dickie, you are an absolute twit sometimes." It was Juliana Popjoy, looking put out. "Rabbiting on like that about him when you ought to have realised that Dorcas has some sort of a thing—"

Mortified, Meg Colveden hastened to exonerate Dickie, who was looking almost comically discomfited. "No, no, it was my fault entirely, Juliana, I kept badgering Dickie with questions. I had no idea Dorcas could hear us and now I could *kick* myself.'' She looked so upset that everybody left in the group rallied to her, including Dickie, all speaking at once.

Sir George patted his wife on the back so heartily that he gave her a fit of hiccups, and asked rhetorically how on earth she was supposed to know. Dickie Nash tried to reassure her on the grounds that Witley had left such a trail of broken hearts behind him that in any gathering including a good many women, the mention of his name would be virtually certain to trigger an emotional reaction in one or very possibly several of them.

Juliana, having regained her equanimity, smiled in a wry, worldly-wise way and pointed out that Dorcas Bookbinder was a grown-up lady perfectly capable of managing her own emotional affairs, and that she'd feel better after a few minutes to herself and a breath of fresh air. She added that if the sight of Blodwen Griffiths behaving towards him in public as she was had made Dorcas see Witley in a new and more revealing light, then that was probably all to the good, and sorry I snapped at you, Dickie my love, and wasn't it about time for dinner?

Miss Seeton took no part in the campaign to cheer Lady Colveden up, for she had unobtrusively wandered off in the American's wake, and was now on the promenade deck. It was a little before eight in the evening, and the *Eurydice* was due to sail at ten. It was reckoned that by then her passengers, well wined and dined, would be in a mood to enjoy the spectacle of the Venetian skyline melting into the velvety night and the sensation produced by a gentle breeze on their faces.

The gangway was of course still in place, and crew members and other functionaries of one sort and another came and went from time to time between the ship and the jetty. Though not particularly large, the brightly illuminated *Eu-*

rydice was also an object of some interest to people enjoying an evening stroll. Miss Seeton waved obligingly down at a family group whose youngest member, a little boy in extraordinarily short trousers, had grinned impishly up at her, revealing a yawning gap where his two front teeth ought to have been.

"Aren't you going to join the others for dinner, Emily?"

Miss Seeton had known that Dorcas Bookbinder was at the rail several yards away, and assumed that if she was disposed to talk she would sooner or later approach.

"I think not, my dear. It has been a long and exciting day, and in any case the waiters, that is to say the stewards, pressed so many delicious canapes upon me that I'm not in the least hungry. At this time of the evening at home, I am beginning to look forward to a cup of cocoa, you know." One must be very tactful. It would never do to allude to her abrupt departure from the party. "I think I begin to understand your remark about moral support now. Oh, *dear*, I had just a moment ago been telling myself *not* to say that. I am so sorry."

"But you were thinking it. Understandably. It was stupid of me to use the expression in the first place."

"If it would perhaps help you to talk about it . . . ?"

Dorcas spun round abruptly and leant with her back against the rail, her elbows propped on it behind her. The attitude drew attention to the graceful lines of her breasts and thighs.

"And even more stupid of me to cause a scene like that."

"A scene? Good gracious, I doubt if a soul apart from those in our own little group so much as noticed you leave."

Dorcas sighed. "You could be right. People were getting sort of animated by then. I hope not, anyway. I don't see why I shouldn't enjoy this trip. After all, I knew they were both going to be on board."

"Professor Witley and Miss Griffiths, you mean."

"Yes. You know, Emily, I thought I was completely over Adrian. And I am, really. I'd also heard that Blodwen was the flavour of the month, so it wasn't as if I was unprepared. But it wasn't easy to watch her all over him like that, and then hear that man Nash saying—"

"Here, use my handkerchief, I always carry a big one."

chapter
~6~

"*GOOD* MORNING, DEAR lady!" Marty Hussingtree trilled the moment Miss Seeton opened her cabin door. "Oh, my, who's an early bird, then?" He tripped deftly past her and placed a tray on top of the desk that doubled as a dressing table. Too late Miss Seeton darted over and tried to cover up the sketch she had been working on before he caught sight of it. Marty peered at it for a moment and then looked up, his lips pursed in a perfect circle and his eyes rolling in exaggerated surprise. "Ooh, aren't you *clever*! You saucy thing, you!"

Miss Seeton quickly managed to retrieve the sketch, which had been inspired by an old favourite of hers in the National Gallery: Bronzini's *Allegory with Venus and Cupid*. The fact that it depicted Cupid caressing the left breast of the naked Venus with one hand while he lowered his lips to hers and supported the back of her head with the other did not embarrass Miss Seeton in the least. It was just that Mr. Delphick and others had so often complimented her on her ability to catch a likeness; and she was simply anxious that Marty shouldn't have too good a look at the faces she had used.

For Cupid was Adrian Witley, whose own hairstyle was in fact uncannily like the one Bronzini had painted nearly

46

four hundred years earlier. Venus, seemingly compliant but in fact having behind his back furtively withdrawn Cupid's arrow from his quiver and being, it seemed, about to plunge it into his wing, had the face of Dorcas Bookbinder. Though half concealed behind a grinning boy-child who somewhat resembled Dickie Nash, Blodwen Griffiths was unmistakably the model for Pleasure, proffering the honeycomb of love while at the same time preparing the sting in her monster's tail. It was an anxious Sir George Colveden who presided over the scene in the role of Father Time, while the masks of comedy and tragedy at the lower right of the drawing looked uncommonly like Ferencz Szabo and Sir Wormelow Tump.

"Just a piece of nonsense of mine," Miss Seeton muttered. Marty smiled with what she persuaded herself was guileless serenity. He had after all seen the sketch for no more than a couple of seconds.

"Must be lovely to be able to draw. Drink your tea before it gets cold, ducky. Oops, I keep doing that and I know I mustn't."

"Doing what?"

"Calling the passengers ducky."

"Well, I, um, that is . . ."

"You are a bit cross, aren't you? I can always tell. I'm ever so sorry. Don't complain to the purser, will you? He's a ghastly old bore. Common as dirt too, I don't mind telling you. Tell you what, can I call you Miss S?"

Miss Seeton smiled at the effusive young man. It was very hard to take offence at anything said by a person who radiated such joie de vivre. "Of course I won't, Marty. And you may certainly call me Miss S if you wish. That's what the computer does, you know. At Scotland Yard, that is. When it sends me cheques."

Marty's mobile actor's features now registered a mixture

of awe and respect, tinged with incredulity. "Scotland Yard sends you cheques? Lucky thing!"

"Just for the Identikit pictures, you know. I hardly deserve it, I do so little, but it is a most welcome supplement. It isn't very big, you see. My teacher's pension, that is. Before I retired, I used to teach art at a girls' school. In Highgate," Miss Seeton added, as though mention of the precise location might add a touch of verisimilitude to an otherwise preposterous story. It, or something, seemed to do the trick. For Marty Hussingtree's features rearranged themselves yet again, and his face became a study in pious reverence.

"*Now* I know who you are," he breathed. "You're her! You've been in the papers! 'The Battling Brolly.' Fancy me not putting two and two together! Ooh, I'm so excited I don't know what to do. Yes I do though," he went on at once, fumbling at the button on one of the breast pockets of his white cotton tunic. He produced a small, battered-looking book with slightly padded covers, opened it, and, frowning thoughtfully, turned over a few pages. Finding the right place, he then offered Miss Seeton the open book. "I thought I'd never want anybody on the page opposite John Gielgud," he said in an emotional way, "but . . . Miss S, can I have your autograph?"

"Well, I hardly—but of course, Marty. If you would really like it." Quite pink with confusion, Miss Seeton signed the book, willing herself not to look at the eminent actor's autograph. It would have seemed somehow, oh, dear, so hard to explain, but . . .

She had never given an autograph to an adult before. From time to time in her teaching days the craze for collecting them had seized the girls, with the time-honoured, dreary old clichés reappearing. "By Hook Or By Crook I'll Be Last In This Book," and "If You Can't Be Good Be Careful." Out of the tail of her eye she could see that Sir

John had no truck with that sort of nonsense, so "Emily D. Seeton" would do very well for her.

"There you are. And now I really mustn't keep you from your work."

Now that he had secured her signature, Marty Hussingtree seemed to have recovered completely from his attack of heroine-worship. He grinned at her cheerfully and favoured her with a wink. "Yes, it's all go today, Miss S. Being all at sea, as you might say. Hustle bustle for us workers. No rest for the wicked."

"Shall we not reach Corfu before nightfall?"

"No, duck—Miss S, I mean. So no walkies today. For you the hurly-burly of the chaise longue, as darling Tallulah put it. Or was it Mrs. Patrick Campbell? Stretch out in the sunshine on deck, go and listen to a lecture if you want to improve your mind."

He surveyed her indulgently, shaking his head slightly from side to side as if still not completely convinced. "The Battling Brolly in person! What a carry on!" Then off with that face and on with a faithful if cheeky retainer expression that made Miss Seeton think at once of Sam Weller. The hoarse cockney accent Marty assumed at the same moment was exactly right too. "Right you are, M'm. Any 'anky-panky or malarkey goes on aboard this ole bucket, yours truly'll pass it on in a brace o' shakes." And finally, when he was halfway out of the door, a batting of the eyelids and a cute female intonation. "Have a nice day!"

Her version of Bronzini's painting stowed safely away with her block of cartridge paper and sticks of charcoal in the capacious shoulder bag she planned to keep with her for the rest of the day, Miss Seeton made her way to the promenade deck. It was a delightful morning, and she felt ready for anything, after such a *very* large breakfast.

What a good idea it was to serve it in what was apparently

called the buffet style, and—even if one had been a little
hesitant at the outset—how nice that passengers were en-
couraged to mingle and get to know each other by sitting
wherever they liked at all meals! So kind of the Bishop of
Bromwich to have come and sat next to one, and introduced
one to Mr. and Mrs. Giles Golightly. Both charming people,
and Mrs. Golightly obviously knew a great deal about the
voyages of Ulysses. Especially kind, as nobody one knew
had been among the comparatively small number of early
risers in the—what was the proper name for it? Dining
room? Restaurant? Saloon, perhaps? Marty would know. A
sweet and obviously talented young man really, even if he
was a little overfamiliar . . . so odd to describe himself as
"resting" when clearly he worked very hard as a steward,
but members of the theatrical profession used many curious
turns of phrase.

"Break a leg," for example. Mr. Jessyp, though as head-
master of the primary school in Plummergen he was not
"in the business," nevertheless "trod the boards" as he
put it. Was indeed a leading light in the Brettenden Amateur
Dramatic Society or B.A.D.S. Jocularly referred to in the
district as the Baddies. And Mr. Jessyp often urged people
to break a leg, explaining without fail every time he did so
that it meant "Good Luck!" in actor's terminology. There
was something about "corpsing," too, which it seemed had
no sinister connotations . . . but one had never fully understood what Mr. Jessyp meant by that. Actors and actresses
must for some reason have a taste for the macabre. Corpsing
. . . break a leg.

"I *beg* your pardon?"

Miss Seeton looked up from the lounger chair in which
she had installed herself to see Juliana Popjoy and Dickie
Nash standing over her. Juliana, glowing with health, was
magnificent in a cherry-red tracksuit embellished with white
stripes here and there. A towel was draped round her neck,

and she looked like an advertisement for some sort of glucose drink or multivitamin preparation. Dickie was also dashingly turned out, being arrayed in well-cut grey flannels, a different blazer from the one he had worn to come aboard, and an open-necked silk shirt. It had to be admitted, however, that in the brilliant Adriatic sunshine he looked a good many years older than he had in the soft lighting of the lounge the previous evening. Well into his fifties, certainly.

"Why, it's Miss Popjoy! And Mr. Nash! Good morning."

"Don't change the subject," Juliana said cheerfully. "What was all that about corpses?"

"Oh, my goodness, was I talking to myself? I *am* so sorry. It is a very bad habit, all too easy to fall into when one lives alone."

"Morning, Miss Seeton." Dickie Nash's face might betray the price of too many years of good living at King's College, but it crinkled into an attractively raffish smile that seemed to speak of a tolerant, easygoing cynicism born of much experience. "I'm all for talking to oneself. You often get a much better quality of conversation that way. We shouldn't have disturbed you, but were a touch alarmed by the mention of breaking legs and corpses. Nothing amiss, I hope?"

"Dear me, no. I was merely musing about the odd expressions theatrical people use."

Juliana gave way to a peal of laughter. "Oh, I *see*. 'The Scottish play' and all that childish nonsense, you mean! And we were afraid you might have had a nightmare!" She looked at Dickie. "Well, if you're quite adamant about not coming for a swim, why don't you sit and talk to Miss Seeton while I do?"

"Would you mind, Miss Seeton?"

"Not at all, I should be delighted."

Dickie Nash settled himself and they watched Juliana lope off in the direction of the swimming pool, which Miss Seeton had noticed earlier. Had she been a swimmer herself she might have been disappointed by its modest dimensions. As it was, she reflected that the average age of the passengers was high enough to ensure that it was unlikely to be much in demand anyway. It was so very pleasant simply to sit on deck and hope to catch a glimpse of the coastline of Italy on one side of the ship, or perhaps one of the islands off Yugoslavia on the other.

"Well, we can look forward to a lazy day. Make the most of it, Miss Seeton. I gather we shall be rushing about like mad things most of the time. So much worth seeing ashore. Which d'you fancy, Sir Wormelow Tump on Ionian decorative art this morning, or the Right Reverend Ashley Bowdler on Greek mythology this afternoon?"

"Oh, both. I had the pleasure of talking to the bishop at breakfast, you see, and I look forward immensely to listening to Sir Wormelow. He is, well, I can hardly claim that he is an old friend, but we have met on a number of occasions. And in a way, he is responsible for my good fortune in being here. They are very fond of each other."

"Who are?"

"He and Sir George. Not forgetting Mr. Szabo, of course. It was his talent for impersonation—"

"Hang on a bit, Miss Seeton, you're leaving me behind. I enjoyed meeting the Colvedens yesterday, but are you seriously suggesting that Wormelow Tump and George Colveden are—"

"Close friends, yes."

"Really? You astonish me, and I'm even a bit surprised to hear Ferencz Szabo's name linked with Tump's."

Belatedly Miss Seeton remembered that details of the attempted theft of the priceless antique Lalique jewelry from Rytham Hall had never been made public. "That is to say, my cottage is only a mile or so away from their house, and Sir George very kindly suggested that the award might take the form of this cruise. Because of Sir Wormelow being one of the lecturers, and it being their wedding anniversary," she babbled. "And for the good of his health. Mr. Szabo's, I mean."

Nash seized on the only point that made any obvious sense to him. "Well, if Szabo's on this cruise for the sake of his health, it didn't begin very auspiciously for him, did it? Almost the first thing Meg Colveden told us when Juliana and I were introduced was that he'd fallen into a canal yesterday and you fished him out. She and Sir George were full of it. It's true, presumably?"

"Poor Mr. Szabo. And the boys hadn't even noticed! Sir Wormelow says they are called *slobberini*, or rather that a friend of his coined the expression, which I must admit sounds disagreeable. But Dr. Bookbinder did, and all three of us naturally did our best to help him, but I had the umbrella, you see, and fortunately it was just long enough—"

"Dorcas Bookbinder was there too?"

"Yes. Such an interesting person."

Nash pulled a face. "I put my foot in it there, I'm afraid. Upset her. I expect you noticed. Oh, talk of the devil. Here comes Ferencz Szabo. Don't say the poor chap suffers from seasickness into the bargain!"

Szabo was making very slow progress towards them, clinging to the rail as if his life depended on it. The effect was distinctly odd, since the sea was very calm and the ship forging ahead serenely. Nash scrambled to his feet and went over to help him.

"Hello, Nash," Szabo muttered. "Give me a hand, will you? I feel like death warmed up." Since, when meeting him previously, Nash had always been treated to the Central European accent that ex-sergeant Frank Taylor had painstakingly relearned on his way up through the antiques trade, and the liberal use of odds and ends of French and Italian that went down so well in Bond Street, he was startled. Nevertheless he offered his arm, and within a few seconds Szabo was installed in the vacant lounger on the other side of Miss Seeton, and doing his best to deal with her anxious enquiries.

"Oh, not too bad really, Miss S. Thanks for asking. A good bit better since I threw up early this morning, if you'll excuse my putting it like that. Must have swallowed a few drops of that revolting canal water after all without realising it." He cast a bleary look across her in Nash's direction. "Apologies, Nash. Don't feel much like being the cosmopolitan smoothie today. And besides, I've got friends on board who know what I talk like in private. Such as Miss Seeton here. So I can hardly use a different voice for each of you, can I?"

After taking this in, Nash smiled at Miss Seeton. "Ah. Now I understand what you meant. Some of it, anyway. She told me you're good at impersonations," he added to Szabo. "So you reckon you'll live, do you?"

Szabo shrugged and pulled a face at the same time. "A fifty-fifty chance, at least."

Nash's face lit up. "Are you a betting man, perhaps? I was thinking of getting up a little sweepstake as a matter of fact."

"What, on my prospects of survival?" Now that he was reclining in comfort, Szabo was brightening perceptibly.

"No, no, on the ship's run until noon today. They always have one on long cruises, but the purser looked at me as if I was off my head when I asked him earlier. Be something to do—oh, hello, Juliana, back already?"

"*Dickie!* Are you trying to work out a way of losing money already?" Juliana raised her eyes heavenward, and then looked down at Szabo. "Hello. Hope you're feeling better. Don't for goodness sake listen to him. He'll bet on anything. I must fly and do something about my hair before somebody takes me for Medusa.''

Then she was gone again, and Nash smiled a little sheepishly.

''I must admit I do enjoy a flutter,'' he said.

chapter

~7~

SIR GEORGE COLVEDEN surveyed the facade of the Royal Palace just off George I Square in the little town of Corfu and nodded in approval. "I think I'd have guessed anyway. Even if that schoolmaster chap hadn't mentioned it over dinner last night."

"What, dear?"

"That the British used to run this place. Fascinatin' to think they still play cricket here. Handsome building, eh? Very fine."

Dorcas Bookbinder consulted her open guidebook. "It was built in 1816 as an official residence for the governors of the United States of the Ionian Islands. Of limestone imported from Malta."

"Exactly what I was explainin', m'dear. Just goes to show. We fixed up a decent water supply for them too, I gather."

"There is a distinct Regency feeling," said Dickie Nash, nodding in agreement. "Actually, this palace or whatever it is rather puts me in mind of the Royal Mineral Water Hospital in Bath."

"Except that Bath doesn't smell deliciously of oranges and lemons, with that lovely hint of herbs. Stop being such frightful pompous bores, you two." Meg Colveden stared

at the two men until her husband at least shuffled his feet
in mild embarrassment. "If you'd paid attention to Wormelow's lecture you'd have found out that the Venetians
ran the Ionian islands long before we did, and for much
longer. Dorcas doesn't want to listen to you boasting about
being British."

During the previous day at sea, Dorcas had not been much
in evidence, and by tacit consent the others had respected
her privacy. Meg was delighted to see that today she seemed
quite to have recovered her poise; and that her own inad-
vertent tactlessness at the welcome cocktail party had been
forgiven, if forgiveness was needed. For Dorcas herself
approached the Colvedens after all the passengers had disembarked for their day on shore obviously happy to spend
time in their company. Then Juliana and Dickie drifted into
their vicinity and the five of them stayed more or less together.

Dorcas merely smiled. "Well, be that as it may," Sir
George huffed. "Are we going to trail round after the
bishop, or take in the sights on our own?"

"I hate being shepherded about," Juliana announced.
"Unhappy reminder of school days. I vote we ask Dorcas
to be our expert guide. What do you think, Dickie?"

"Absolutely. Much more fun than being under starter's
orders all the time."

"Would you mind, Dorcas?" Meg asked.

"I'm flattered, but you have the wrong idea, I'm afraid.
I'm an art historian. I don't know a thing about Corfu."

"Ah, but you've got a guidebook," Sir George said cun-
ningly. "And we've all signed up for that optional jaunt
this afternoon to the unpronounceable place over the other
side. So—"

"Palaeokastritsa."

"There you are! Must be an expert, you know how to
say it. So since we're all going to be on parade later on, I

think we should take it easy this morning. Potter about by ourselves." He looked hopefully in the direction of a cluster of little bars and taverns. "Might try a spot of the local tipple in due course, eh? *Ouzo*, they call it. Not bad at all. Don't care for the resinated wine though. Tastes as if you could strip paint with it. Right, that's all agreed, then, and you're in charge, m'dear. Where to first?"

"Well, according to the book, the church and tomb of Saint Spiridion would be a good place to start."

"Keep him on the premises, do they? Okay by me," Dickie said, and Juliana poked him in the ribs.

"Dickie, for a Byzantine historian you make an excellent barbarian," she chided him. "Behave yourself, or I shall go and join the bishop's flock after all."

As the little group followed Dorcas along the esplanade, Sir George tugged at his wife's sleeve, lagging a little behind.

"I say, Meg," he whispered hoarsely. "Don't want the American gel to hear this, bit touchy on the subject, you said. But did you happen to notice where that blighter Witley went?"

"Who?"

"Witley. Got to keep an eye on him, you see."

Noticing that Dorcas was in animated conversation with Juliana and Dickie and most unlikely to overhear, Meg replied in more normal tones. "I didn't, I'm afraid. He certainly isn't with the main crowd. And why should you want to keep an eye on Adrian Witley?"

Her question was disingenuous. In fact Meg was piecing together for her own edification a remarkably accurate theory to account for the not-very-mysterious hints and evasions her husband had been indulging in ever since Ferencz Szabo had unexpectedly decided to join the cruise. She didn't expect an answer to her question, nor did she get one.

"Damn nuisance Miss Seeton went off with Wonky and Frank like that. Safer if we all stick together, I'd say."

"Safer? Good heavens, George, you're not fussing over Miss Seeton again, are you? She couldn't be better protected than with those two to look after her."

"Don't know about that," he persisted gloomily. "Look what happened last time she and Frank joined forces. He ended up in something little better than an open sewer and she had to fish him out. Take it from me, if we'd been in charge of Venice too, we'd have sorted out their drainage problem in no time. I knew a chap once, colonel in the Royal Engineers he was . . ."

Bickering amicably, they moved on and soon caught up with the others.

"No it wasn't. It was pathetically incompetent," Carlo Crivelli said. "And the main reason why I sent you that note instructing you to meet me here was to tell you so in person."

He and Witley were already on the western side of the island, at the promontory known as Palaeokastritsa. A good many of the cruise passengers were due to go there in the afternoon. They would be taken there by bus: Witley had been obliged to find a taxi, and he made the journey in so foul a mood that the beauty of the country along the route was completely lost on him. It was hard to remember that until very recently Crivelli had treated him with at least the appearance of courteous respect. Until delivering that dreadful, stomach-lurching ultimatum in Venice. And now he was speaking insultingly polished English and treating him like some sort of lackey.

Anger mingled with self-pity flared up in him. Everything seemed to be falling apart. No wonder he'd been offhanded with Blodwen when she turned up at his cabin door uninvited yet again the previous night, obviously planning a heavy session. After all, the first night, after they sailed, had been a total disaster. But instead of getting the message when he reluctantly tried to oblige her, and hardly surprisingly in the circumstances failed to rise to the occasion for the first time in years, the stupid creature had been glutinously "understanding." Last night she'd no doubt seen as an occasion to show off a few different tricks and prove just how irresistible she could be when she put her mind to it.

Well, he'd sent her off with a flea in her ear all right, and didn't expect to be bothered again by Blodwen bloody Griffiths. Not until after he'd got this awful Szabo business off his mind, anyway. Then he might be disposed to give her another whirl. Or take up one or more of the other offers bound to come his way.

"Listen, Charles, I don't take kindly to all this talk about 'instructing' me to do this, that, and the other," he said. "I'm not at your confounded beck and call. Who the hell do you think you are, anyway?"

The Italian smiled, and when he replied it was in silky-smooth tones of the utmost reasonableness. The effect was infinitely more frightening than his previous grim expression had been.

"Do you really want to know, Adrian? Then I'll tell you, because I certainly wouldn't want you to labour under any misapprehension. I am the man who is here to ensure that you solve our little problem by disposing of the inconvenient Mr. Szabo before the end of this cruise. And do, please, think up something more likely to have the desired effect than shoving him into a canal barely ten feet wide and practically in front of friends of his. Friends able to go to his assistance within seconds. You probably succeeded in giving him diarrhea, that's all. Following that fiasco, you wasted a whole day yesterday while we were at sea, and lost a useful opportunity. Because you were on the right track in one respect at least in Venice. Szabo's told people in my hearing that he can't swim, and that he's terrified of water. Never mind, there are alternatives here on dry land."

Crivelli turned, and with a dramatic gesture pointed up at the castle of St. Angelo, poised on a peak high above the monastery outside which they were standing. "I've been up there myself. It isn't an easy walk, but well worth it for the view when you get to the top. The track's quite tricky in places, and you need to watch your step. A man—Ferencz Szabo for instance—could easily lose his footing and fall, oh, two or three hundred feet, perhaps." He sighed, took a snowy handkerchief from his trouser pocket, and dabbed delicately at his brow with it before continuing.

"I don't know why I should bother to do your thinking for you, but you may wish to consider inviting Szabo to go up there with you this afternoon. For a frank private conversation. To sort things out, you know, in a man-to-man way. While the others are being shown round the monastery." He smiled again, with his lips only. The shadowed eyes remained expressionless.

"They have a fine twelfth- or thirteenth-century ikon of the Virgin Mary there. You won't want to miss it, so if I were you I'd pop in and have a look at it while you're waiting for the party from the *Eurydice* to arrive. I can confirm that Szabo has put his name down for the trip, by the way. I checked before I left the ship this morning."

What little was left of Witley's self-control finally snapped. "Will you *shut up*, damn you, Crivelli! Now you listen to me for a change. I must have been mad to take the risk I did in Venice. Thank God nobody spotted me, and thank God I didn't succeed. I've had a bit of time to think since then, and I can tell you this. I've learned my lesson. If you seriously think I'm going to make any further attempt to kill Szabo, you're out of your mind."

• • •

"Oh, miles better, thank you, Miss Seeton. It certainly wasn't very amusing at the time. But you know, in a funny sort of way it might have cured me of my phobia. I felt ghastly most of yesterday, but I'm sure that was because of a bug I picked up from the canal water. The idea of being on board a ship didn't bother me at all. And when I began to feel better I realised that being on a cruise has its definite plus side. I'm enjoying myself now."

"I am so very glad. And you do indeed look quite your old self again. Doesn't he, Sir Wormelow?"

"I beg your pardon?"

"Miss Seeton reckons I look my old self again, Wonky. Do pay attention."

"Ah. Yes, I s'pose you do."

"You're a bit distrait yourself today, old man. Anything wrong?"

"No, no. Not in the least."

"Good. Because it was your idea to come and look at this awful casino place."

"It isn't awful, is it, Miss Seeton? It's surrealist if anything, a bit before its time. And it wasn't planned as a casino, hang it. It was built for Elizabeth of Austria back in the early nineties."

"Well, I think it looks as if it was built for Walt Disney."

The three of them were standing in the gardens of the palace, contemplating the enormous modern statue of Achilles that gave the whole property its name of Achilleion.

"Well, it's very *interesting*," Miss Seeton offered, rather dubiously, "but I must admit that I expect to enjoy the visit to the monastery this afternoon rather more."

"Oh, by the way." His voice sounded slightly cracked, and Tump cleared his throat and began again. "Sorry. I was just going to mention that I've decided to play truant from the optional tour this afternoon. I've, um, remembered that I've got some lecture notes to prepare. So I'll duck out of lunch and slip away now, if you don't mind.''

"What a pity. But that makes us all the more grateful to you for giving us the pleasure of your company this morning. Doesn't it, Mr. Szabo?''

"Yes indeed,'' Szabo hastened to say. "Off you go, Wonky, and do your thing. We'll wander back to the bus and find the Colvedens, and tell you all about the monastery this evening. Mind how you go.''

Miss Seeton caught Szabo's eye as they made their way to the waiting bus for the two-mile ride back to Corfu town, where they had been urged to visit the museum before the second bus ride of the day for those who had opted for the additional excursion to the monastery at Palaeokastritsa. "You know, Mr. Szabo, I must confess that you made me want to laugh. When you mentioned him. Walt Disney, that is. Such a very apt comment, if I may say so. I see you are still amused at the thought yourself. I'm delighted to see you in such a good humour again.''

"Thank you. Yes, I'm in a very good mood now. Life does have its amusing side, doesn't it?''

In fact the Frank Taylor aspect of his nature was uppermost at that moment, and he was hard put to it not to laugh out loud. Because he had realised something that Miss Seeton hadn't. Namely, that Wormelow Tump had become distracted and then abruptly decided to excuse himself from the remainder of the programme ashore immediately after Szabo himself had caught a glimpse of the steward Martin Hussingtree some distance away in the gardens.

The young man was looking extremely smart in tight white trousers and a pale blue shirt of Byronic cut. He was wearing also a winning smile, and waggling the fingers of one hand shyly but invitingly in Tump's direction.

chapter
~8~

IF, MISS SEETON reflected, one had not been so fascinated
by the sight of an aged monk pottering about in the garden
of the monastery at Palaeokastritsa, one would not have
lagged behind the others as they followed the Bishop of
Bromwich inside. In that event one would probably not have
noticed that Professor Witley had appeared apparently from
nowhere—for one surely would have remembered had he
been on the bus—waylaid Mr. Szabo, and engaged him in
conversation in spite of Mr. Szabo's evident lack of enthusiasm for his company.

How very satisfying it had been, therefore, to see Mr.
Szabo shrug his shoulders after a little while and set off
with Professor Witley up the steep, stony track that must
lead to the ancient castle high above. They were going for
a walk together. A very good sign. That Professor Witley
was unhappy about the antipathy that Mr. Szabo had hinted
at, well, more than hinted at, over tea at the Ritz; and that
he was anxious to effect a reconciliation.

Certainly he seemed to be weighed down by anxiety.
Professor Witley, that is. Because his shoulders were
slumped and he looked back two or three times as they
mounted the track. No doubt he was wondering whether a
stiff climb all the way to the summit on such a warm after-

noon was such a good idea after all. He was still quite a young man, of course, but sadly out of condition. Perhaps if all went well and he returned in a happier mood, one might make an opportunity to raise the subject of yoga, and suggest that he might consider taking it up. In the course of general conversation, of course. As a splendid way for a person leading a sedentary life to keep fit.

On second thoughts, why not on the way down? For they did have two full hours here before the bus was due to leave for the return journey to the ship. No doubt the gentlemen had agreed to pay their own visit to the monastery later on, and admire the famous ikon at leisure after the majority had already seen it. And there was much to be said for such a plan. If one were to follow their example—at a discreet distance, of course, so as not to intrude upon their privacy—one might find a pleasant little vantage point about halfway up the track, and encounter them, as it were, on their way back.

Not that Miss Seeton doubted her own ability to reach the summit. Daily yoga practice over a period of some years might not have enabled her to master some of the more advanced postures. These, all the authors of the popular manuals agreed, should not in any case be attempted by those past the middle years of life. Nevertheless, the exercises had done wonders for both her leg muscles and her lung capacity, and Miss Seeton was modestly aware that she could outwalk most people many years her junior.

When she set off, at least ten minutes after Witley and Szabo, it was therefore in a sprightly fashion, and indeed at a cracking pace. The two men remained out of sight for several minutes, but then Miss Seeton rounded a hairpin bend and realised that she had gained on them rapidly. Some thirty yards ahead, Ferencz Szabo was negotiating a rocky slope with great caution, and justifiably, since the track was unfenced and a few feet to his right there was a sheer drop.

Adrian Witley followed a couple of yards behind. Thus, both men had their backs to her and needed to concentrate on what they were doing far too hard to think of looking round.

Realising this, Miss Seeton was all the more alarmed to see that Witley appeared suddenly to be seized with cramp or some other sort of muscular spasm. At least, he suddenly reared up, his back arched, and flung his arms forward. Miss Seeton made haste to go to his assistance, but by the time she had reduced the distance between them to a few yards he seemed to recover, lowered his arms slowly, and resumed his laboured progress, even gaining ground on the neat but corpulent little figure of Ferencz Szabo.

When Witley again arched his back and swayed forward, arms outstretched, Miss Seeton realised it was time for her to act decisively if he was not to topple over the edge, possibly even carrying Szabo with him. Quickly reversing her umbrella, she lunged forward and managed to hook the handle into the open collar of Witley's shirt and haul him back to safety. Well, more or less, because he toppled and fell heavily on to his side, uttering something between a wail and a yelp of anguish as one ankle twisted under him.

"Oh, my goodness, Professor! Do forgive me, but there was no time, you see, and you were in imminent danger of losing your balance and bumping into—"

"Yes. And he did lose his balance, didn't he?"

Miss Seeton looked up at Szabo, disconcerted by the coldness in the voice of one she had always thought of as being essentially a good-humoured, even genial man.

"Hello again, Miss Seeton. You seem to be making a habit of coming to my rescue. A habit I'm deeply grateful for."

"Oh, no, I assure you, it was Professor Witley who was—"

"Making heavy weather of things? Yes, so I gather."

Szabo extended a dainty shoe—quite unsuitable footwear for climbing rocky mountain tracks—and nudged the whimpering man at his feet none too gently in the ribs with it. "Get up, Witley, you're not hurt," he then barked in what struck Miss Seeton as being an unnecessarily harsh manner. Then he stepped over his erstwhile companion and courteously offered Miss Seeton his arm. "Perhaps we should go back and join the others."

"But, but we must help—"

"Oh, I think we can leave Professor Witley to make his own way down. It isn't all that far. Please, Miss Seeton." The pressure on her arm was very firm, his manner insistent. "Do come."

"Hello, what have we here, then? The walking wounded turned up at last, eh?" Sir George watched with interest as Adrian Witley came into view, limping and stumbling the last hundred yards to the gangway of the *Eurydice*. His shirt was dirty, his trousers torn, and he looked deeply depressed. "Can't mistake Miss Seeton's handiwork, can you?"

There was still an hour before they were due to sail, and he, Tump, and Szabo were sitting at a table outside a nearby tavern, cloudy glasses of ouzo and water before them.

"Thought I'd never manage to collar you two alone for a bit of a chinwag," he went on. "Especially when you came down that path with a face like thunder and nearly bit my head off, Frank."

"Bugger would have very likely killed me if good old Miss S hadn't turned up in the nick of time and weighed in with her umbrella. Hardly calculated to put me in the sweetest of tempers. Damn it all, George, how would you have liked it? Sorry, all the same. Shouldn't have snapped at you." He glanced at Tump, who was stretched lazily back in his chair, the picture of relaxed contentment. "How was *your* afternoon, Wonky?'' he enquired pointedly. ''Lecture notes all, um, buttoned up?''

''Yes, thank you. A most satisfactory couple of hours.''

''That's good. We've both earned a drink, then.''

Colveden suddenly sat bolt upright. ''I say, Frank, you don't mean that seriously, do you? I mean, you don't really think Witley was *trying* to shove you over the edge?''

''Good grief, man, I've just been telling you he not only tried, he damn nearly succeeded.''

''But according to Miss Seeton, it was Witley that nearly got killed. Spasm of cramp or something, and she hauled him away from the edge by the scruff of his neck.''

''Spasm of cramp my foot. Spasm of attempted murder, more like.'' Szabo drained his glass and turned to beckon to the waiter for a refill. Colveden caught Tump's eye.

''D'you believe him, Wonky?''

''I wasn't there. But I'd believe almost anything of Adrian Witley,'' Tump said, and stifled a yawn. He spoke again as Szabo turned back to them. ''Particularly in relation to Frank here, who's made a monkey of him in London. Thoroughly nasty piece of work, is friend Witley.''

''By Jove, you're spot on there, you know. That gel of his, the droopy one that was winding herself round him at the cocktail party the other night, you know who I mean.''

''Blodwen Griffiths.''

''That's her. Collects stamps or something, Meg was explaining.''

''Not stamps. Ancient coins. And she doesn't collect them, she lectures about them.''

''Extraordinary way to make a living. Not at all bad-looking, either. Anyway, what I was about to say is this. When you and Miss Seeton came sauntering down the path as large as life, there were quite a few of us standing around. All struck by the sight of Witley trailing a long way behind you, practically on his knees and looking like something the cat's brought in. Even I felt a bit sorry for the chap. Said as much to that nice young American woman who happened to be standing alongside. She did, too, I could tell. Went rather white and twitched a bit, as if she was inclined to go and lend him a hand. Well, this stamp or coin woman of his actually did. Rushed up to him wailing endearments.'' Sir George paused and frowned.

"Made a bit of an exhibition of herself, quite frankly. But then she's Welsh, isn't she? That would account for it. But do you know what? The bounder just shoved her away, practically knocked her over, and swore at her for good measure. We all heard. Even the bishop. Not at all the sort of thing he's used to, I should think, though you'd be surprised what I've heard army padres come out with in my time. Well, I can tell you, nobody felt sorry for Witley after that. Surprised she didn't slap his face. Disgraceful behaviour, humiliating a lady in public like that. All the same, Frank, it's a bit much to go about accusing people of attempted murder.''

"Have it your own way, George. But I'll tell you one thing, if I ever have a private conversation with that man again, it'll be at my instigation, not his.''

Miss Seeton made her preparations for bed, lay down to sleep, and switched off the bedside light. The *Eurydice* had sailed, and the slight rolling of the ship was by no means disagreeable. Technically, the Aegean Idyll was about to begin, for soon they would leave the Adriatic. Two islands tomorrow: Patmos and Samos. And after such a full day on Corfu!

She sighed. Poor Professor Witley. One couldn't possibly approve of the ungentlemanly way in which he had rebuffed his lady friend, but all the same, one did still feel a little uneasy about Mr. Szabo's rather callous attitude after the unfortunate confusion on the mountainside. A pity that those who had been on the excursion to the monastery all seemed to want over dinner to give their own conflicting accounts of what they thought they had seen to those who had not. Naturally one had turned aside all direct questions and, thanks to dear Dorcas who had been sitting at the same table, managed to bring the conversation round to the beneficial results of the practice of yoga.

Mr. and Mrs. Golightly, alas, were very sceptical, but Mr. Crivelli had seemed most interested, even to the point of asking one's own views on the points put so well by Dorcas in her wonderfully enlightening explanation of the philosophy at the heart of the practice. So nice that Mr. Crivelli had chosen to sit next to her. A most erudite man, and with a face that reminded one of . . . what *was* the painting in which she had seen Carlo Crivelli's face before, or a face very like it?

Of course! Lotto's well-known portrait of Andrea Odoni! Put Mr. Crivelli into a fur-lined gown, and imagine him with a full, soft beard, and he would be Andrea Odoni to the life. And what a fascinating coincidence that Mr. Crivelli should himself be a distinguished collector and connoisseur of antiquities, like Lotto's subject. Was he perhaps descended from the painter of the same name? The fifteenth-century Vittore Crivelli, that is? It seemed quite possible, given Mr. Crivelli's interests. Now, here was a little test of memory. How well could one recall the background Lotto had painted? The "props," as Mr. Jessyp would call them, that he had provided for his subject? Or more likely that the subject had himself chosen from his collection?

Her imagination moving into high gear and now much too wide awake to think of sleeping, Miss Seeton switched on the light again, rose from her bed, and sat at her little desk-cum-dressing table. Her drawing materials were to hand, and before long Carlo Crivelli was coming vividly to life in the guise of Andrea Odoni.

chapter

~9~

AMELITA FORBY KNEW she looked good that day. She liked to think she looked pretty good most days, but had taken particular pains over her appearance in honour of the occasion, because she seldom had reason to visit New Scotland Yard.

The reason for applying her warpaint wasn't that she hoped to catch the eye of the Metropolitan police commissioner, who had within the past hour or so been giving his customary press conference following the publication of the annual report on crime statistics for the capital. It was because she knew that the man the tabloid newspapers inevitably called London's Top Cop would be flanked by several of his senior officers. In view of the subject under discussion, these would be certain to include her old friend Chief Superintendent Delphick; and Delphick was duly on parade.

It was not the first press conference of its kind that Mel had attended. She knew therefore that it was Delphick's practice, after the commissioner and his immediate entourage withdrew, to linger behind and make himself available to fill out, informally and unattributably, the background to the report. As the *Daily Negative*'s star feature writer Mel had a right and indeed a duty to go along. She planned, if she could talk him into it, to bear Delphick off afterwards for a bite of lunch and a private chat.

She had no reason to think that "The Oracle," as he was known to all, was a susceptible sort of man. Nevertheless, she liked and respected him, and thought it only proper to try to look her best. Clearly she made the desired impact, because after he eventually indicated that enough was enough and that it was time for the ladies and gentlemen of the media to be going about their business, it was Delphick himself who crossed over to her during the hubbub of their departure and laid a hand on her arm, treating her to one of his rare warm smiles.

"Hello, Mel. Good to see you here. You turned what promised to be a dismal chore into a positive pleasure. I had something nice to look at while His Nibs was philosophizing."

"Thank you for the compliment. You look very dashing yourself today, Mr. Delphick. I'd quite forgotten you'd be in uniform for the occasion. Tell me, are you allowed out on the street like that? I was going to invite you to have lunch with me if you're free."

"Not really, and yes, in that order. I am free and I'd be delighted to have lunch with you, provided we talk about anything other than crime in the metropolis. But I must ask you to bear with me while I slip up to my office and change. It would, I fear, inspire alarm and despondency in your average restaurateur or publican if I were to march into his premises got up like this. Not to mention his patrons, who might think a raid was being staged. Mind studying those elegantly prepared charts on the wall for five minutes? I can't believe you need to attend to your stunning appearance."

"Flatterer."

Delphick was as good as his word, and when he rejoined Mel it was as the familiar nondescript but somehow reassuring man in a well-worn, comfortable-looking tweed suit rather than the imposing senior police officer with the double row of medal ribbons above the left breast pocket of his tunic. Ribbons, Mel had learned with surprise from a chain-smoking hack sitting beside her during the conference, that attested to the fact that their owner had not only got about a bit during World War II, but in the process had been awarded the Military Cross and been made an officer of the Order of the British Empire, military division.

Now they were sitting in an Italian restaurant in Victoria Street no more than two or three hundred yards from New Scotland Yard. It called itself a trattoria, and uniform or no uniform Delphick had been greeted by name by the head waiter who had ushered them to a table for two in a quiet corner. Delphick had with courteous firmness made it clear that he and not Mel was paying: that much as he might like to, he could not with propriety accept the hospitality of a well-known journalist with a substantial expense account.

Accepting the inevitable with good grace, Mel had also very much enjoyed the meal and a spirited conversation about the decision to admit women students to four previously all-male Oxford colleges, but not just yet, the attitude of members of the Royal Family to the recently widowed Duchess of Windsor, and the shock resignation of Home Secretary Reginald Maudling. After all that, Mel accepted a second cup of coffee from the hovering waiter and sat back, replete.

"That was absolutely delicious. The pasta, the veal parmigiana, everything. No offence, but I'd rather assumed you were a roast beef sort of person. The upstairs dining room of a suitably gloomy pub."

"That's because we've only ever eaten at the same table in Plummergen. And the cuisine at the George and Dragon inclines to the hearty rather than the exotic."

"You can say that again. You know, I almost hate to do

this after you've entertained me so handsomely . . . but, what are you up to with her, Mr. Delphick?''

"Whom can you possibly mean?"

"You're the one that brought Plummergen into the conversation. Miss S is who I mean, that's who.''

Delphick winced. "Since you are my guest, I will pass over that appalling example of Fleet Street syntax, and admit that I did guess that you were referring to Miss Seeton. Miss Seeton is, so far as I know, enjoying a well-earned holiday. Why do you ask?''

"Because Thrudd and I have been away ourselves for a couple of weeks. Out of touch.'' Mel was not given to blushing, but she did pause for a moment, looking a little like a kitten that had been at the cream. "And after I'd gone back to work and sorted through all the bits and pieces waiting for me at the *Negative,* I thought I'd give the Battling Brolly a call—''

"I do wish you wouldn't call her that.''

"—but there was no answer. So I rang Mrs. Bloomer to leave a message for her.''

"Oh, dear.''

"You may well say oh, dear. Mrs. B was full of it. About how Miss Seeton has gone off on a cruise to Greece.''

"She'll enjoy that, I'm sure.''

"With Sir George and Lady Colveden.''

"Better and better. They get along splendidly.''

"And Sir Wormelow Tump.''

"Really? What a coincidence!''

"And Ferencz Szabo.''

" 'Curiouser and curiouser,' said Alice. Or was it Pooh Bear?''

"At the expense of Scotland Yard. Mrs. Bloomer had got the idea into her head that the trip was some sort of prize.''

"Mrs. Bloomer is a good soul. Salt of the earth, as they

say, but misinformed, I fear. Alas, Scotland Yard doesn't give away prizes. Could the Colvedens have invited her along?''

"Now come *on*, Mr. Delphick! I've known you too long to be fobbed off with a story like that. And you should know me better than to hope I'd be taken in. You may not have a very high opinion of the *Daily Negative*—''

"On the contrary, I like to think I am among your most devoted readers.''

"Why, thank you, kind sir. Anyway, we have our methods when we want to find things out. In fact it was simplicity itself to call St. James's Palace and get hold of some flunkey who told me that the said Tump is currently a guest lecturer on board a cruise ship operated by Heron Halcyon Holidays. And the most cursory glance at that estimable company's current brochure—good grief, you've got me talking like you—what I mean is, I only had to flip through it to see that Tump's not the only guest lecturer. They've signed up Adrian Witley too.''

"Miss Seeton will be able to avail herself of every luxury that money can buy, evidently.''

"Mr. Delphick, I don't have to spell it out, do I? Remember, you're talking to, among other things, the *Negative*'s Art and Saleroom Correspondent.''

"Good heavens.''

"Now I admit there isn't a lot of interest among our readers in your run-of-the-mill stuff. The price fetched by an eighteenth-century commode, a silver tureen, or even an important sedan chair isn't likely to get my editor excited.''

"I imagine not.''

"But if one of Nell Gwynn's nighties were to go under the hammer, that would.''

"It takes all sorts to make a world, Mel,'' Delphick said, in a charitable way. "A colleague of mine who specialises in these matters tells me that Queen Victoria's drawers are in steady demand too."

"I don't doubt it. Anyway, let me mention something else that would put a twinkle in my editor's eye. A really first-class libel action involving a TV star and a top Bond Street dealer in antiquities and fine art objects. Such as my contacts in certain circles suggest is brewing between Adrian Witley and Ferencz Szabo."

"Do they, now?"

"Yes, they do. And that being so, two things strike me as being very fishy. First, that Szabo should have—voluntarily, I assume—paid good money to go on a cruise featuring Adrian Witley as one of the lecturers; and second, that you should have arranged for Miss Seeton to go along for the ride."

"In that case, all I can say is that your high intelligence, undoubted beauty, and charm of manner contrast sharply with your nasty suspicious mind. And, since I have a mind that is even nastier and more suspicious, I dare to add that in all probability you are now about to try to blackmail me."

Smiling sweetly, Mel nodded. "Got it in one. You see, even as it stands, this would fetch very good money—or the promise of useful favours to come—if I were to pass it to one of the smart gossip columnists on another paper. It would of course probably wreck your scheme, whatever it is, but that's life. However, I'm not going to do that, Mr. Delphick."

"Of course not. Provided, that is . . . ?"

"Provided that you come clean with me. Because if Miss Seeton is about to pull off another one of her feats, I want the whole story as an exclusive for myself."

Delphick sighed ostentatiously. "You're a hard woman, Forby. I'm rather tempted to call your bluff, you know. Because I have no scheme, as you put it. However, you have cheered up my day for me, so I'll tell you off the record that Miss Seeton is on board that cruise ship at George Colveden's request, not mine. Yes, I've heard that an ancient chunk of sculpture has been temporarily withdrawn from an auction sale because Szabo questioned the authentication Witley provided, and that there's some sort of a storm in a teacup as a result.''

"I'm impressed."

"We have our methods too, you know. I will continue. Details of the remuneration Miss Seeton receives as an occasional consultant to the Metropolitan police force are confidential, and under no circumstances will I discuss them. As I said when you first mentioned her name, so far as I am concerned she is enjoying a well-earned holiday. She will take pleasure in the company of her friends, I'm sure, but it is most unlikely that she even knows, much less cares, about the quarrel between Witley and Szabo. That'll be patched up in any case before long, I expect. Libel actions are notoriously chancy, and they'll both back down when it comes to the point, or agree to a settlement out of court.''

Adrian Witley had decided not to go ashore at either of the two islands at which the *Eurydice* called on the day following the visit to Corfu. In fact he remained in his cabin, brooding over a number of things. These included his humiliation on the mountainside, the foolish public display of ill temper towards Blodwen Griffiths, which had resulted in a near total boycott of his lecture in the evening, the agonising dilemma that faced him as a result of Crivelli's ultimatum, and his own physical woes. His wretched ankle *was* sprained, and though the ship's doctor had strapped it up, he had done so with distinctly untender hands, and with an expression on his face that announced very clearly that like everybody else on board the doctor had heard about his caddish behaviour and thoroughly disapproved of it.

After the long run overnight from Corfu to the Dodecanese, most of the passengers were looking forward to
their undemanding day of island-hopping. Patmos and its
monastery with the grotto reputed to be the setting for the
Revelation of St. John occupied the morning, and Samos
the rest of the day.

Absorbed in the contemplation of his troubles, Witley
was only vaguely conscious of the comings and goings of
the passengers as they passed his cabin, and had no idea
where the ship was, or indeed of the time, when he suddenly
realised that somebody was knocking on his door. By then
he was in a condition to welcome almost any distraction,
so he called out.

"Come in. It isn't locked." The door was opened, and
Witley regretted issuing the invitation as soon as he saw
who his visitor was. "Oh, no, not you! Look, for heaven's
sake, I'm in no condition to discuss *anything*. I'm in pain
and I'm thoroughly fed up. So there's no need to close the
door like that, just go away and leave me in peace, will
you—what the devil are you doing with that? My God, have
you gone crazy or something? I . . . *Stop it! No!*"

If he had been able to get to his feet in time, Witley
might have managed to defend himself, but he wasted val-
uable seconds by looking wildly round for something he too
could use as a weapon.

After the first blow he was capable only of groaning.
After the second he was silent, and after the third he was
dead. Only when satisfied that this was the case did Witley's
murderer listen intently at the door before opening it an inch
or so, peep out to confirm that there was nobody else about,
and then quietly depart.

chapter
~10~

It was the steward Marty Hussingtree who eventually reported Witley's death, after he went to tidy his cabin while most of the passengers were either ashore or at dinner on board in the evening. Returning to his own cabin after the meal, Wormelow Tump found Marty standing white-faced in the corridor outside, tearful, shuddering, and incoherent. Tump summoned the purser, and after a while Marty managed to explain that something had happened to Adrian Witley, but not precisely what. That was established beyond question after they went in procession to Witley's cabin, where it became immediately obvious to the purser that they required if not the urgent services, then certainly the official presence of the ship's doctor.

The doctor needed to make only a cursory examination to satisfy himself that Witley was beyond medical aid. He therefore gave a couple of tablets out of his bag to Marty, explained that they would calm his nerves, ordered him to keep his mouth shut—after taking them, of course—and go off duty forthwith. He requested Tump, much more politely, to refrain from mentioning what he had seen to any other passenger, and offered him tranquillisers too; but Tump declined and took his leave, having no intention of withholding the stupendous news from his friends.

Using his passkey, the purser locked the cabin door behind them with the body inside, and he and the doctor then reported to Captain Mungo Macallister, who uttered a series of colorful oaths. In the course of his seafaring career, Macallister had more than once been required to cope with the consequences of the death of a passenger, but not, so far as he knew, one who had been murdered. And the doctor was in no doubt whatever that Adrian Witley had met his death by violence at the hands of some person other than himself.

Captain Macallister had no urgent desire to see for himself, so he confined himself to a few questions, nodding approval when the doctor assured him that he had instructed both Hussingtree and Tump to keep quiet about what they had seen. He then in turn enjoined silence on the doctor and the purser, and retired to his own quarters to commune with his folder of standing orders and emergency instructions. He had barely begun when he heard a great thundering on his door. Fearing that he was about to be told of some new disaster, he jumped up and opened it, to be confronted by Sir George Colveden, who was pop-eyed with excitement.

"Just heard the news about Witley, Captain. Realised you'd need me so I came at once. Vital to brief you in confidence, my dear feller."

Macallister recoiled, recovered quickly, and told himself that no matter what the provocation, he must try to convey calmness, composure, and reassurance. Inwardly he was seething. Heard the news, had he, by God? Damn and blast all blathering, loose-tongued, empty-headed passengers! Was it possible it was all over the ship within ten minutes at most? It would have been too much to hope that the affair could be hushed up altogether, but it ought to have been possible to keep it quiet until well into the following morning. Hell's teeth! And who was this pompous old fool with his talk of "briefing in confidence," anyway?

"Forgive me, sir. I should remember your name, but with more than two hundred passengers . . ."

"Colveden. Major-general, retired. Justice of the Peace, Ashford Magistrates' Court in the County of Kent. My services are entirely at your disposal, Captain."

"Colveden . . . oh, aye, of course. Sir George Colveden." Calm the old boy down, that's the thing. Can't have him barging round upsetting other passengers who might not have heard. "Well, that's very good of you, Sir George, but everything's under control, I assure you. Professor Witley's accident—"

"Accident? Accident my foot! Blighter's been murdered—"

"Please, there's no need to raise your voice . . . come in, sit down, and let me shut the door. Now then, what's all this talk about murder?"

"Not suggesting he bludgeoned himself to death falling out of bed, are you? Should have put you in the picture at the outset, I s'pose. Knew there was trouble brewing."

"Picture? What picture?"

"Warned you about this Witley. A bad lot, you know. That sort generally come to a sticky end one way or another. Puts me in mind of old Jumbo Wagstaff, chap I knew in the army years ago—but I mustn't run on about him now. No time to lose, you see. You must get a what d'ye call it, radio message, off to Scotland Yard at once."

"A what? To where?"

"London. Scotland Yard. I just told you, dammit. Whitehall 1212 the phone number used to be in the old days, but it's all different now. Anyway, your signals boffin will know how to raise them, I expect. Chief Superintendent Delphick's the man to ask for, but I should think he's packed up for the day by now. If he has, they can get hold of him and get him to ring you back, no doubt. Fortunately I've

got one of his people on board already, so we can kick off
the investigation while we're waiting for Delphick to get
here—''

"Sir George. I have already explained that everything is
under control. I'd be obliged if you'd return to your cabin,
and—what was that I heard? Did you say there's a British
police officer on board my ship?''

Sir George raised a warning finger to his lips, and then,
since it was conveniently placed for the purpose, used it to
brush his moustache while he directed a meaningful look
at the captain.

"No names, no pack drill, old boy,'' he then said in
lowered tones. "Under cover, d'you see. Not at liberty to
divulge the, um, person's identity. Not a police officer in
the ordinary sense of the word, anyway. Expert consultant,
you might say. Planted on board on my advice, with the
approval of the top man at Scotland Yard. Commissioner
in person. So you can rest assured Delphick'll beetle out
here at the double to take care of everything, as soon as he
gets the word. Don't forget to mention my name, there's a
good chap.''

Captain Macallister goggled at him. First a murder, and
now a raving madman. Babbling about undercover police
agents planted with the connivance of Scotland Yard. Next
thing, this unmitigated nuisance would be complaining that
the Archbishop of Canterbury was pumping poison gas
through his keyhole. Perhaps if he could be persuaded to
go quietly back to his cabin the doctor could give him a
sedative. Have to be humoured in the meantime, of course.

"Yes, yes, absolutely,'' he said warily. "I'm greatly
obliged to you for telling me all this. Now I mustn't keep
you any longer from your bed, Sir George. As I said a wee
while ago, I have everything under control—''

"Under control? Under control? With a murderer running

loose? And why the devil are you blithering about going to bed, sir? It isn't even half past nine yet!''

"Now, now. Calm yourself. I shall be notifying the nearest British consul and the Greek authorities——''

"*What?* You aren't seriously proposing to let a lot of unshaven Greek policemen swarm about a British vessel on the high seas, are you?''

"We aren't on the high seas. We're in Greek territorial waters, moored for the night at Samos.'' How the dickens did this lunatic know that if the *Eurydice* had in fact been in international waters, Scotland Yard would indeed have been responsible for the investigation of Witley's murder? But that was by the way. Of course the local police must be informed; but not necessarily right away, come to think of it.

The *Eurydice* was due in any case to sail in the general direction of Piraeus the next day. It might well be that Heron Halcyon Holidays would, when word of the murder got back to London, decide that the cruise would have to be truncated. Arrange for the passengers to be disembarked at Piraeus, offer them an alternative shore-based tour of famous sites on the mainland for the rest of the time they'd paid for. Something like that.

And although this red-faced Colonel Blimp type was obviously stark staring bonkers, there might be something to be said for keeping the local police out of it for a while. Better perhaps to get in touch with the consular people at the British Embassy in Athens in the morning and let them liaise with the Greeks at a senior level than to try to organise anything at night in this remote little backwater much nearer to Turkey than Greece. The pensive expression on the captain's face was lost on Sir George, who continued in full spate.

"You're splitting hairs, Macallister. Dash it all, you've no more idea when Witley was clobbered than I have. Could easily have been while we were out at sea. Tell you what, let me talk to Delphick myself. He's a good fellow, very quick on the uptake.''

Sir George stopped abruptly, and his face fell. "Unless it's got to be in Morse code or something. Never did get the hang of that very well," he confessed. "I was astonished when my son Nigel got a badge for it in the Scouts, you know. Or was that semaphore, perhaps? I must ask Meg."

"Now just ye listen to me, Colveden," the captain said grimly, aware that he was rapidly approaching the end of his tether, and allowing much more of his native Glaswegian accent to show through. "I'd remind ye that I am in command o' this ship. An' I'll no' be in need o' lessons in how tae do my duty. Off awa' wi' ye now, an' dinna be soundin' off tae all an' sundry aboot what ye may or may not know."

"Ah. Fair enough, old boy, you're the skipper, and I was out of order, eh? Right ho. Mum's the word. Talk to Delphick yourself, by all means. That's D-E-L-P-H-I-C-K, by the way. Give him my regards, will you? I'll leave you to it then, and just rummage about a bit on my own. Start drawing up a list of suspects, you know.''

"Ye'll do no such thing, d'ye hear . . .'' But Sir George didn't hear. He had departed as precipitously as he had arrived.

Meg Colveden was sitting with Miss Seeton in the otherwise deserted lounge when her husband sauntered in, his hands buried in his trouser pockets and his head slightly upraised, while from the way his lips were pursed, he seemed to be whistling almost silently to himself. She knew that exaggeratedly debonair pose of his: it told her that he was either up to no good or about to embark on some clumsy attempt to pull the wool over her eyes.

"*There* you are at last, George! Where on earth have you been?''

"Been? Me? Haven't been anywhere. Ah, hello, Miss Seeton. Haven't seen much of you today."

"George, answer me. I haven't seen you since Wormelow Tump drew you aside just after dinner. He looked as if he'd seen a ghost. What was it he whispered in your ear that made you look so peculiar and promptly disappear?"

"You're right, Wonky didn't look frightfully well, did he? Something he ate, perhaps."

"And there's something very odd about the atmosphere on this ship this evening. Miss Seeton agrees with me."

"That would be because most people have gone for a stroll on shore. I say, do either of you happen to know how to use Greek telephones?"

"George, if you attempt to change the subject once more I swear I shall scream as loudly as I can. There must be somebody within earshot. In the meantime, stop looking around you so furtively, sit down and tell us what is going on."

"Oh, very well. You're bound to find out pretty soon anyway. I was just wondering how to put it, as a matter of fact. You know that bounder Witley?"

"Really, George! Of all the idiotic questions—"

"Course you do. Silly of me to ask. Well, he's, um, well, not to put too fine a point on it, dead, actually."

"Oh, dear, I had a feeling that this day would end badly," Miss Seeton said, not sounding in the least surprised. "I was quite unable to achieve the proper frame of mind for my yoga practice." Meg remained silent, one hand to her heart, gazing from one to the other of them wide-eyed.

"Yes, well, I've just been having a bit of a yarn with the captain about what's to be done. On the taciturn side, like a lot of Scotsmen, you know, but I think he has his head screwed on reasonably well. Canny, that's one of their favourite words, isn't it? Well, this fellow's pretty canny, I'd say. Only problem is, I'm not too sure that he's grasped the importance of doing things in the right order, which is why I thought I might go ashore and try to get through to him myself, you see. Only it could be a bit tricky, trying to handle it through a Greek telephone operator.''

"Get through to whom, George?"

"Why, Delphick, of course. You've met Delphick several times, Meg. Let me think, he was last in Plummergen when his man Ranger married Dr. Wright's gel.''

Again Miss Seeton seemed unsurprised by what she was hearing, and even nodded judiciously. "It all turned out so well in the end, didn't it? A beautiful wedding. There is no doubt that this is a case of murder, then?"

"Oh, not the slightest. As I've just been explaining."

"But, George, you *haven't* been explaining," Lady Colveden almost wailed. "I know perfectly well who Mr. Delphick is, but what's he got to do with Adrian Witley?"

"Ah, well, Wonky Tump actually saw him, you see. I didn't. Very upsetting for Wonky. In his cabin, you know. Witley's, I mean. On the floor in a heap." He cleared his throat in an embarrassed way. "Hardly a pleasant thing to mention in the presence of ladies. Nasty business altogether, in fact. Blunt object, that sort of thing, I gather."

"Oh, how dreadful! Who on earth could have wanted to . . . ?"

"That's exactly what we want Delphick to come and sort out. I can take care of a good deal of the spadework—sorry, unfortunate choice of word—I mean, I can draw up a list of suspects to have ready for him when he arrives. Thought I'd make a start right away, as a matter of fact—"

"Sir George, he is definitely, the captain, I mean, going to notify him? Mr. Delphick, that is."

"Well, I jolly well hope so! I made it perfectly clear to him that it was the first thing to be done. Talked him out of some silly notion he had of calling in the local bobbies.

Preposterous! Shouldn't think they speak English, for a start.''

"I rather doubt if Mr. Delphick speaks Greek, if it comes to that, George."

"That's beside the point. Which is that having gone to all that trouble to arrange for Miss See—hrumph, that is, what I meant to say is that I'd feel happier if I could get a message off to Delphick meself. What do you think, Miss Seeton, eh?''

"You will think me very persistent, but may I ask again, Sir George, did the captain actually say he would send a message to Mr. Delphick?"

"Well, not in as many words, I must admit. To tell you the truth, he got rather shirty with me. Gave me a bit of a dressing down, actually. So I thought I'd make a tactical withdrawal and see if I could find you. Spot of consultation in order, I thought. What do you think I should do?''

Miss Seeton began to gather her things together. "I think we should all go . . . ashore is the word, isn't it. And go to one of those bar places,'' she said. "Find an English-speaking waiter and ask him to help us either to put a call through to London or to dictate a telegram over the telephone. But if I may venture to suggest it, perhaps we should speak to Miss Forby. I understand that she works at her newspaper office until quite late in the evening. She will be most interested and could then explain things. To Mr. Delphick, I mean." Miss Seeton smiled sweetly at Sir George.

"Just in case your advice slips the captain's mind.''

chapter
~11~

SIR HUBERT EVERLEIGH carefully removed his glasses, buried his head in his hands for a few moments, then rubbed his eyes, replaced the glasses, and looked wanly at Delphick. "I haven't had enough coffee yet. Nevertheless I am not going to ask if I heard you aright," he said. "I have no doubt that when you tell me that a reporter on the *Daily Negative* telephoned you at home yesterday evening, I may take your word for it. Nor am I altogether surprised that the reporter concerned is Amelita Forby, in whose company you were observed leaving these premises after the commissioner's press conference yesterday morning. You have, I feel sure, an entirely satisfactory explanation to offer to Mrs. Delphick should she seek one."

"Unnecessary, sir. My wife took the call and seized the opportunity to indulge in some minutes of what she refers to as 'girl talk' with the lady. She has met both Miss Forby and her, how shall I put this, cohabitee. The gentleman in question is at least twenty years younger than I am, and even in my own opinion much better-looking."

"Good. Then that just leaves this trivial matter of Miss Forby's message. To the effect—do correct me if I'm mistaken—that Miss Seeton is on or near an island in the Dodecanese, that she is investigating the murder of Adrian

Witley, the television personality, and that she would be grateful for your assistance."

"Flattering in a way that she should ask for me, sir, wouldn't you agree?"

Everleigh sat back and blinked a few times, signalling that the preliminary pleasantries were over. He now looked both serious and displeased. "Delphick, have you taken leave of your senses? Do you seriously expect me to believe a word of this farrago of nonsense?"

"Let me put it this way, sir. I believe it."

"Be serious, man. The woman's having you on. One of these hoaxes the gutter press go in for."

"I beg to differ, sir. I think it extremely responsible on Amelita Forby's part to have rung me. Many reporters in Fleet Street would have tried to get the story splashed all over the front page without a second thought. But she got in touch with me at once to let me know what she thought she had been told. I put it like that because she explained that there had been a good deal of static on the line from Greece. Furthermore, she mentioned to me that Sir George Colveden had given the impression of being in an excitable state of mind throughout the conversation."

"I thought it was supposed to be Miss S who'd rung her."

"No, sir. It was Colveden. It seems that he regards himself as being in charge of the investigation, but he did say that Miss Seeton was already busy making drawings that would no doubt make everything crystal-clear."

"The man's mad, Delphick. I've always said so. And to think you sent poor Miss Seeton off to spend a week in his company!"

"Um, on your instructions, sir."

"Yes, well, never mind that now. Anyway, even granting it was Colveden on the phone, this Forby woman surely didn't swallow everything he said hook, line, and sinker, did she?"

"No, sir. She suggested to me that I might wish to enquire discreetly whether the holiday tour company had heard anything from the captain of the cruise ship, and undertook to take no action until Colveden's information had been confirmed in some way."

"And?"

"I got hold of their operations manager. It's true, sir. Adrian Witley has been murdered. A short time before I spoke to him, a radio telephone message had been received from the ship, reporting Witley's death by violence on board at the hands of a person or persons unknown, and asking for urgent instructions. The operations manager seemed to think I must be psychic. He had to consult with his directors, of course, and got back to me very early this morning."

"Delphick, it is *still* very early this morning. You were lying in wait for me when I arrived, remember? All right. Let's begin again, shall we? On the assumption that there must be something in this extraordinary tale. First question. Why did Colveden or Miss S or whoever it was ring Amelita Forby of all people?"

"Because Miss Seeton thought that the master of the ship ought at least to have the chance of notifying us through official channels, as Colveden said several times he'd instructed him to do. But they wanted to make sure I got to hear about it one way or another. They know from experience how efficient Mel Forby is."

"Colveden had instructed the . . . ? Why in the world should Colveden take it upon himself to tell the captain to do any such thing?"

"He argued, apparently, that the crime might quite possibly have been committed while the ship was in international waters. Whereas the captain seemed to be in favour of reporting it to the Greek police and letting them take charge.''

''Good Lord! Fancy old Colveden knowing about that peculiar legal quirk.''

''He takes his duties as a magistrate very seriously, sir. It's a hobby of his to ponder the fine print in legal textbooks, I'm told.''

''Just on the off chance that a lay magistrate from the depths of Kent might find himself faced with a case of murder on the high seas?''

''Well, it seems that's exactly what he thinks he is faced with, so perhaps he hasn't been wasting his time after all,'' Delphick pointed out. ''At all events, he seems to have sown enough seeds of doubt in the captain's mind for him to have put off informing the Greek authorities pending receipt of guidance from London.''

''And what guidance has he been given?''

''A couple of hours ago he was ordered to make for Piraeus, the port of Athens, with all speed. The ship should arrive there some time this afternoon. Before nightfall, anyway. Arrangements will be made for the passengers to leave the ship and be accommodated in a hotel for the time being. Meantime the British Embassy is being put in the picture through the Foreign Office here, and asked to establish contact with the Greek police. Whether or not George Colveden has a legal point, it's clear that the Greek authorities must be involved. So should we, sir. I believe that both our embassy and the Greeks would welcome that. In short, I should like your permission to go, sir.''

''All joking aside?''

''Yes. I judged it both fair and prudent to get back to Amelita Forby and inform her in confidence that independent confirmation of Witley's death had been received. I asked her to keep the matter strictly to herself for the time being, and she agreed. She will without question hold her tongue for as long as possible, if only to ensure that hers will be the biggest and best story, but she certainly won't allow herself to be scooped. She plans to fly to Athens later today in order to be on the spot when the news does break.''

''Will the cruise company cooperate?''

''They've agreed to make no statement at least until the ship reaches Piraeus. If something like this had to happen, it's fortunate that it came to light in the evening, in an isolated place. Gives us a few hours to get organised. But by tomorrow at the latest the news of Witley's death is bound to leak out. He's not newsworthy internationally, but he's a big name in this country, so the British media will descend en masse. Especially when it emerges that Miss Seeton's somewhere in the picture. Mel Forby will probably have spiked their guns by then. Even so, I'd very much like to have talked to Miss Seeton and to Colveden by the time the matter becomes public knowledge.''

''I see your point. Whether or not it's strictly speaking any business of the Metropolitan Police, people are going to think it is. We don't want to be made to look fools. All right, Oracle, you'd better get your skates on and leave me to do the paperwork to get it all authorised. Is there a scheduled flight reasonably soon, or do you want top brass to try to get the RAF to fly you direct from Northolt?''

Delphick looked at him in astonishment. ''Would you really go so far as to do that, sir? I'm . . . I'd be very grateful.''

There was a hint of a smile on the assistant commissioner's face as he reached for the telephone. ''Hasn't it occurred to you yet that we take rather a lot of notice of your advice, Oracle? And think very highly of Miss Seeton, needless to say. If she has let it be known that she requires your services, we must deliver you to her side with all possible speed.''

•   •   •

"Morning, Miss Seeton. Hope I'm not too—what are you doing here, young man?"

"Good morning, Sir George. Marty has just brought me some tea. It was particularly kind of him, because the poor boy still isn't feeling at all well."

Marty Hussingtree did look pale, and was perceptibly drooping, but he managed a sick little smile. Sir George stared at him in bafflement for a moment longer, and then snapped his fingers as enlightenment came to him. "Got it! You're the young feller who found him! Witley, I mean. I say, thought's just occurred to me. Sorry, bit indelicate, I'm afraid, but if he's still in that cabin I hope to goodness somebody's been bright enough to set the air-conditioning to maximum." He was just in time to catch Marty when he swayed, and lower him into a chair.

"Put your head between your knees, old chap, you'll be as right as rain in a minute," he advised bluffly, before turning to Miss Seeton. "Apologies for bargin' in, but we ought to make a start, d'you see. Thought you'd be up and about by now. I've just found out from the purser that we're going full speed ahead, bound for Athens. For some reason Captain Macallister said he couldn't see me when I banged on his door. In the shower, perhaps. The purser wasn't all that helpful, either. Cagey sort of man, didn't want to tell me really, but I winkled it out of him. Had no idea I'm an experienced interrogator, you see. I've had to crack a lot tougher nuts than him, I can tell you. Anyway, to come to the point, I've drawn up this list of suspects to discuss with you, Miss Seeton. Before we start grillin' 'em, you know."

"Sir George? I wonder . . ." Miss Seeton shyly indicated the steward, who was just beginning to show signs of life again. "Perhaps we should let Marty get on with his work? If he feels well enough to do so, of course?"

"By Jove, yes, I'd quite forgotten he's one of—that is, all right now, young man? Good. Nothing to be ashamed of, you know, my boy. Even guardsmen pass out during long parades now and then, if they forget to rise up on the balls of their feet every so often. Works like a charm, you know. Learned the trick myself as a young subaltern and never had a bit of trouble after that. Right, off you go, then.'' Sir George nodded genially as Marty drifted out of the cabin, but as soon as the door was closed he hung his head shamefacedly.

''Put my foot in it there, I'm afraid. Because he is, isn't he? A suspect, I mean.''

''I do wonder if it is quite in order—''

''I put him on my list quite early on.'' He took a piece of paper out of his pocket, unfolded and scrutinised it. ''Here he is—'Steward who found body. Query motive.' I've had to put 'Query motive' beside one or two others, actually. Wonky Tump, for example. But take Frank Taylor, he's a much better bet. Listen. 'Claims that W'—W stands for Witley, d'you see, saves time writing it over and over again—'Claims W tried to kill him on mountain. Also worried about possibility W might sue him.' Then there's—''

''Surely not, Sir George? Can you really think that either Sir Wormelow or Mr. Szabo—''

''Old Frank? Not for a moment! Nor Wonky. Got to put them both down, though. Fair's fair. I have excluded you, Miss Seeton, by the way. And Meg. Not her style at all.''

''Thank you,'' Miss Seeton said rather weakly, and braced herself with a sip of tea.

''Then there's that fine-looking Popjoy woman and her friend. Nash. Let me see, now. Yes, here we are. What I've written beside their names is, 'Nash claims W poo-poohed antique in Popjoy's shop, antique bought by Italian collector who sold it at big profit.' Not too sure that would drive either of 'em to go so far as to murder him. Might, I s'pose, depending on the size of the profit. Now, *cherchez la femme*, as the Frogs say. There's the Welsh gel, obviously fond of W, can't think why, but the cad treated her atrociously that afternoon. Blodwen Griffiths. I've put 'Hell Hath No Fury Etc.' beside her name, rather neat, what? Now, some of the others. I suppose one ought to rule out the bishop, more or less ex officio—hello, who can that be?''

The tapping on Miss Seeton's cabin door ceased, and a voice could be heard outside. "Emily? Are you there, Emily?''

"Come in, Dorcas! Good morning. Sir George was just leaving.''

"Was I? But I hadn't . . . oh, I see. Beg your pardon, Miss Seeton. Morning, m'dear.''

"Hi. Am I intruding, Emily? We did say seven-thirty for a yoga workout, didn't we?''

"Yes. I'm quite ready, and looking forward to learning that new posture you mentioned.''

Sir George frowned first at Dorcas, and then at his piece of paper, before reluctantly folding it up and stowing it away. "Yes, well, mustn't get in the way. We'll get back to this later on, then, shall we?'' He glanced again in a more friendly fashion at Dorcas Bookbinder. "Apologies, m'dear. Got rather absorbed. We've just been goin' through a list of suspects I've drawn up, before tryin' to work out who killed Adrian Witley . . . I say, give us a hand, Miss Seeton, I think she's fainted.''

chapter
~ 12 ~

THE GREAT MAJORITY of the passengers on board the *Eurydice* arose that morning still unaware of the demise of Adrian Witley, but by the end of breakfast time nearly all had heard the news. The dining salon was abuzz with it, and among the participants in what had been advertised and sold as an Aegean Idyll a great variety of emotions were manifested.

Since several differing accounts of the manner of Witley's death were current, none of them accurate but all lurid, it was hardly surprising that respectable horror predominated; and many normally hearty eaters decided that toast and coffee would suffice that morning. Solemn or appalled expressions were by no means on display at all the tables in the dining salon, however. A good many passengers tucked in with unseemly relish, making return trips to the buffet for second helpings, and gossiping animatedly both there and when they sat down again. There was an unworthy tinge of schadenfreude about the remarks of some of those who had, either secretly or fairly obviously, resented the fact that an academic had achieved fame and, presumably, riches as a star of television. A few bold spirits even suggested aloud that, shocking though his fate had been, of course, Witley had been asking for it.

The absence of Blodwen Griffiths was generally noted, and Miss Seeton feared that the situation might be getting a little out of hand. She was sitting unobtrusively at a table in the corner of the dining salon with an open book in front of her. She had observed that this was a ploy used at breakfast time by a handful of passengers who were evidently disinclined to be chatty early in the day, and found that it was most effective in discouraging casual approaches. She was relieved when authority intervened in the form of the purser, who entered the salon and mounted the small dais at its far end.

A tall man who looked lugubrious at the best of times, he twitched and fidgeted in what was obviously acute embarrassment as a hush fell over the assembly and all eyes were turned towards him.

"Er, ladies and gentlemen," he muttered, almost inaudibly even in the expectant silence. "If I could have your attention—"

"Speak up, please! Can't hear you!" It was Dickie Nash, on behalf of the majority, it would seem, since his intervention was accompanied by murmurs of support.

"*If I could have your attention,*" the purser now bellowed in a reedy tenor, before finally achieving a reasonable mezzo forte, "for a moment. I have to inform you that due to certain circumstances beyond our control . . ."

"He means 'owing to.' Not 'due to.' I cannot abide sloppy English," murmured a stringy man with a prominent Adam's apple who was sitting near Miss Seeton, and who had previously been immersed in a critical study of the plays of Sophocles.

". . . a change in the cruise schedule. Instead of calling at Delos and Mykonos today we are proceeding direct to Athens."

The purser gamely attempted to continue, but had to give way in the face of the babble of protest and questioning that greeted this announcement. He simply stood there shaking his head mutely until eventually he was able to make himself heard again.

"Captain Macallister requests all passengers to please assemble in the main lounge at nine-thirty, when he will make various announcements with regard to, er, this. Oh, yes, and the lecture by Dr. Blodwen Griffiths scheduled to begin at ten A.M. has been cancelled."

"Deplorable. The man has no idea how to construct a sentence," the student of Sophocles grumbled, and closed his book with evident regret.

It was eight forty-five when the purser made his escape from the dining salon; and neither he nor any of the other ship's officers seemed to be available for the next three quarters of an hour, at least in person. Two announcements were however made over the public address system, at nine and nine-fifteen A.M., and the main lounge was almost full several minutes before the appointed time for the captain's promised address.

"Don't mind us joining your little mutual protection society, I hope?" Dickie Nash asked as he and Juliana Popjoy slid neatly into two vacant chairs immediately behind the Colvedens. "It's just that since the cocktail party the first evening Juliana and I like to think we're honorary associates."

"Ah, morning, old boy. Not at all. Delighted. Be glad of a word with you both afterwards, actually. You know our friends Wormelow Tump and Ferencz Szabo, of course?" They were sitting to Sir George's right, while on Meg Colveden's left was a tense, white-faced Dorcas Bookbinder, with Miss Seeton guarding her other side. Since the Bishop of Bromwich was on Miss Seeton's left, Dorcas could scarcely have had a more impressive bodyguard. While the two newcomers were greeting Tump and Szabo, Sir George addressed them both in a stage whisper.

"The American gel's taking it rather hard, for some reason. Thought I'd better let you know."

Whatever she might be thinking, and notwithstanding her pallor, Dorcas looked perfectly dignified. Blodwen Griffiths, who now put in an appearance on the arm of Mrs. Golightly, did not. As Mrs. Golightly solicitously settled her in an easy chair hastily vacated by her husband, it was plain for all to see that the numismatist was in a piteous state. Her hair was a mess, her eyes were puffy, and she held a handful of paper tissues to a nose that was reddened and evidently runny.

"Poor creature. No, look the other way, George. She must feel dreadful, and certainly doesn't want to have everybody staring at her."

"Can't help that, Meg. Matter of evidence, you know. Tell me, would you say she looks as if she's got a guilty—"

"Shut up, George! Anyway, here's the captain."

Captain Mungo Macallister swept into the lounge, flanked by his first officer and the purser. Presumably because of the solemnity of the occasion, he and his deputy were dressed not in the whites that they and the other officers had been sporting ever since the first day at sea, but in the formal navy blue uniform he had worn to greet the passengers at the welcome cocktail party on the evening they embarked. They made the purser, who had not changed, look slightly frivolous by contrast, in spite of the gloom of his expression. Some passengers were so impressed that they half rose in their seats, but the captain waved them down again with a most expressive movement of his right hand. It conveyed appreciation of their courtesy, coupled with a stern recognition of the fact that the circumstances were such that the niceties of etiquette might be dispensed with.

"Bishop Bowdler, ladies and gentlemen. I must begin

by thanking you all for assembling here at short notice, and apologise for the inconvenience to which you have been and, I regret to say, will continue to be subjected.'' The tough Glaswegian accent with which he had almost succeeded in cowing Sir George Colveden the previous evening was barely perceptible. It had been replaced by a polished, officer-class assurance softened by the merest suggestion of the heather and the lochs, of shortbread and smoked salmon.

''Many of you have already been informed that I have given orders for a course to be set that should result in our arriving at the port of Piraeus late this afternoon. I am aware that in the past hour or two a great many rumours have been circulating about the reasons for this change. I therefore asked to see you all so that I may have an opportunity to pass on to you such information as I have.'' Captain Macallister removed his hat from under his arm, gazed pensively for a moment at the gold braid adorning its peak, and then placed it carefully on the lectern behind which Adrian Witley had stood two nights earlier to confront an insultingly meagre audience.

''It is my melancholy duty to inform you all that a death has taken place on board. That of our distinguished guest lecturer, Professor Adrian Witley.'' Macallister's poise was still intact, but his accent was slipping. His pronunciation of the word ''melancholy'' had been that of an elder of the kirk, and there was more to come.

''This would in any case have been a deeply distressing occurrence. It is rendered all the more so by the circumstances, which are such that the doctor canna cairtify the death as being due to natural causes.''

This information came as no surprise to anybody in the lounge, of course, but nevertheless provoked a most satisfactory frisson.

''Accordingly, I have been in communication with the authorities, and have received urgent instructions. These are that we must with regret abandon the cruise as such." Up went his hand, but it took the captain several moments to recapture the attention of his audience.

"But not, I hope, your holiday. It is hoped to arrange an alternative programme for you, based on a hotel in Athens, and I am authorised to advise you that the possibility of compensation is under consideration."

At this a forest of hands shot up, and the hapless Macallister knew that the awkward questions were about to be asked. Even so, it seemed to him to be worth an attempt to avoid answering them.

"I canna answer any questions now—"

"But you must, Captain!" It was Juliana Popjoy who spoke, though "spoke" is a pathetically inadequate word to describe the use to which she put a thrilling contralto voice with plenty of volume to it. It put one in mind, Meg Colveden was to remark long afterwards, of Edith Evans as Lady Bracknell in *The Importance of Being Earnest*, quizzing poor Miss Prism. "You have just informed us in a roundabout way that Adrian Witley has been murdered."

"Weel, now, I never said anything aboot murder—"

"Nonsense, of course you did." Juliana was now on her feet, all eyes upon her. It wasn't only her remarks that were impressive. So were the effects of her deep breathing on her bosom, splendid even in repose. "And you then proceeded to try to pull the wool over our eyes by offering us all outings in Athens!"

"I think I shall have to strike her off my list," Sir George muttered sotto voce, leaning over to his wife. "Don't think she'd come out with something like that if she'd done for Witley, do you?"

"You spoke of communication with the authorities, Captain, but you omitted to specify them. Be good enough to do so." Miss Seeton turned to see who had made this latest interjection, and was not altogether surprised to discover that it was the Sophocles man who disapproved of the purser's grammar. She nodded in satisfaction: in these lax times he for one knew how to shape a sentence.

Captain Macallister drew himself up stiffly. Fierce women with statuesque figures put a man off his stride, but self-important pedants were another matter entirely. "I trust you'll accept my assurance as master of this vessel that all the appropriate official procedures are being obsairved," he said, icicles hanging from his words.

Sir George lumbered to his feet. "Yes, no problem there," he affably informed the assembly. "Captain Macallister and I talked it over, and I persuaded him—"

"*Sir George!* Be silent, confound ye! Ye're oot of order an' I'll thank ye tae hold yer tongue." With a visible effort the captain brought himself back under control. "These proceedings are now at an end. Any further instructions will be announced over the public address system."

Macallister swept out, forgetting his hat; but this was picked up by the first officer, who rather hesitantly followed, the purser bringing up the rear. Still standing, Sir George seemed to realise that he had the floor, and instinctively milked his big moment for all it was worth. He shook his head sadly at the doors through which the officers had disappeared, and then turned back to his fellow passengers.

"Understandable, you know. Under a lot of strain, poor fellow. Something snaps, words spoken in the heat of the moment, seen a lot of it in my time. Anyway, you can take it from me that Scotland Yard has been put in the picture. It's a hundred to one their top CID man's on his way to meet us—"

"You're on!" Dickie Nash said. "For a tenner."

"Really, Dickie, at a time like this!" If Colveden was enjoying the limelight, Juliana showed no inclination to be upstaged. She rose again and surveyed the other passengers, many of whom by now looked thoroughly bemused.

"The thing is, people, that if Adrian Witley has been done in, I don't see how they can let us off the ship at Piraeus or anywhere else. Because a murder implies a murderer, and that person is on board. Almost certainly in this room."

Given that those present were almost all of above-average sophistication and intelligence, the number who seemed not previously to have made this simple deduction was surprising. Miss Seeton was not, needless to say, among them. She employed the time, until the initial hubbub that followed Juliana's declaration died down a little, by studying the faces that most interested her.

"She's absolutely right, you know," Sir George roared after a while, making so much noise himself that everybody else subsided. "But there's absolutely no need to panic," he went on in a more normal manner. "Investigations are well advanced, and I think it safe to say that a certain expert from Scotland Yard who is already among us will be in a position to identify the culprit within a matter of hours. Enough said, what? So let's make the best of things. Suggest you all go off and amuse yourselves now."

"Oh, dear," Miss Seeton said, as the implications of Sir George's breezy remarks seemed to sink in, and people looked around and at each other with expressions ranging from unease to suspicion and simple alarm. Miss Seeton looked on as the other members of what Dickie Nash had dubbed the mutual protection society stood up and clustered round the Colvedens.

Wormelow Tump looked grimmer than she had ever seen him, and when she caught Ferencz Szabo's eye she noticed how hard and forbidding he seemed. The quality of relentlessness she had observed in him when he had refused to assist Witley on the mountainside was much in evidence. Juliana Popjoy was still queenly and determined, arguing about something with Dickie Nash, and Dorcas Bookbinder now appeared to have regained the inner strength that had so impressed Miss Seeton when they first met.

Sir George cleared his throat to command their attention. "Right, now what I suggest is—"

"Not now, George," Szabo said, so coldly that everybody else turned their heads to stare at him. "I don't think any of us is either qualified or in the mood to play detective. Certainly not poor Miss Seeton. You must have embarrassed her quite enough already. If you really do have reason to suppose that the British police are likely to become involved in this affair, I think you should leave it at that. I'll see you all later."

Szabo's unceremonious departure had a chastening effect, and he was soon followed by Dorcas, Juliana and Dickie, and Wormelow Tump in that order. When even Lady Colveden murmured something about powdering her nose and slipped away, it seemed at last to dawn on Sir George that there was a general lack of enthusiasm for his ideas.

"I say, Miss Seeton, frightfully sorry if I said the wrong thing. Just assumed you'd come up with the goods as always if we all chewed the fat a bit before Delphick comes aboard."

"I'm afraid you flatter me, Sir George. Perhaps it would be wiser on the whole to . . . if you will forgive me, I think I should like to go to my cabin."

"Absolutely. Been pretty upsetting for you, I expect. Tell you what, I'll go and have a word with the bishop. Might persuade him to lay on some sort of memorial service, just to pass the time. I don't suppose they have a bugler on this kind of ship, do you? Pity. I always feel that sounding the Last Post is a good way of seeing a chap off, even a civilian . . ."

Since Sir George seemed to be happy enough to occupy himself with this new project, Miss Seeton left him to his musings and made her way out of the lounge. Really, Sir

George meant well, but was inclined to . . . a bull in a china shop, that was the expression, though really it was in the highest degree improbable that a bull could ever find itself in such a—unless in India, perhaps, where bulls were sacred. And cows. What, one wondered, would be the legal position of the owner of an Indian china shop who tried to bar a sacred cow from entering his premises?

By the time she arrived at her cabin, Miss Seeton had almost forgotten why she had decided to go there, and was generally in a state of some confusion. She was certainly too confused to register more than the fact that as soon as she opened her door, a gloved hand grabbed her arm and she was dragged in, whereupon the masked owner of the hand flung a blanket over her head.

After that she knew only darkness, a darkness that became more profound before long. For no matter how hard she struggled, Miss Seeton failed to dislodge the hands that choked her into unconsciousness.

chapter
~13~

"THERE SHE IS, I think. Yes, I can just make out the name from here," Mel Forby said, and Delphick sighed with envy at the sharpness of her eyes. He saw only a good-looking, white-painted ship some distance away, slowly approaching but not yet obviously heading for the jetty on which they were standing.

There was a considerable reception committee waiting for the *Eurydice* to come alongside, and Mel was lucky to be there. When she turned up at the British Embassy in Athens, her press credentials had been viewed with nervous suspicion by Harold Withers, a surprisingly seedy-looking man with a red nose who was nevertheless a second secretary in the consular department. Fortunately for Mel, Delphick had beaten her to it, thanks to some fast work on the part of Sir Hubert Everleigh and a crony of his in the Ministry of Defence.

Delphick had been flown to Athens in a neat little RAF executive jet, met by the British Air Attache, and had a brief meeting with the embassy's political counsellor before being passed on to Withers, who was to escort him to police headquarters, where he was of course expected. Delphick had taken a firm line with Withers, explaining that Miss Forby was expected, that she was present in a personal capacity as a close friend of Miss Seeton who was a passenger retained as an expert consultant by Scotland Yard, and that she would accompany them. Delphick knew from experience that, with or without his cooperation, Mel would find out whatever was worth knowing. He knew also that, treated with courtesy, she could be persuaded to handle the story in a way calculated to be helpful to Scotland Yard. Besides, she *had* been the one to make sense of Colveden's no doubt confusing telephone call and pass on the information, and he owed her for that.

The Greek police officer assigned to the case—a handsome man who rejoiced in the name of Xenophon Papagiannis and spoke excellent English—was clearly under the impression that Mel was the close friend not of some passenger or other but of Delphick himself, and embarrassed both of them by winking conspiratorially and making gallant remarks to the effect that he too was occasionally able to combine business with pleasure, but not as often as he would like.

A romantic Captain Papagiannis might be, but there was nothing unprofessional about the arrangements he had made in the few hours between that initial meeting in Athens and their arrival at the quayside in the port of Piraeus. Police barriers had been erected to prevent unauthorised access to the ship, and of course to make sure that none of the passengers slipped away. A van contained the gear that would be used by the scene-of-the-crime experts who were standing by, and an ambulance was parked discreetly, ready to convey the corpse of Adrian Witley to the mortuary as soon as it had been photographed in situ.

The harbourmaster was in attendance, as was the local representative of Heron Halcyon Holidays, a plump, bald-headed Greek with a soup-strainer moustache. Delphick realised that this gentleman undoubtedly had plenty to look harassed about, but suspected that he always looked as if he were about to burst into tears of despair. He explained plaintively that it had not been possible to reserve rooms for all the passengers in one hotel. They would have to be distributed among three. Never mind, Captain Papagiannis reassured him. All passengers and crew would in any case be required to remain on board during the preliminary stage of the investigation.

Papagiannis had already accepted with a philosophical shrug the assertion of his distinguished colleague from Scotland Yard that it ought to be possible to sort out the sheep from the goats fairly quickly. The passports of everybody aboard the *Eurydice* would have to be impounded for the time being, Delphick agreed, but insisted that the great majority could probably be allowed to go to their hotels after a while.

Privately, the Greek police officer wondered why both the stolid Englishman and the attractive young woman he took to be his *petite amie* were quite so confident that a short list of suspects could be drawn up so quickly, but was content to wait and see. If Scotland Yard really had planted their mysterious "consultant" Miss Seeton on board in the expectation of trouble, and she was as efficient as they claimed, perhaps the whole affair really could be cleared up without fuss.

"Yes. It is the *Eurydice*. In ten or fifteen minutes we should be able to go aboard," Papagiannis said. "I will put my men to work at once, and then, Chief Superintendent, we will speak with the captain."

"No, Sir George, you listen to me," Captain Mungo Macallister said firmly. "In a few minutes I shall need to be on the bridge. We're due at Piraeus before long. I tell you frankly that last night I thought you were talking through the back of your head. But it seems that somehow or other Scotland Yard has become involved in this matter. I've been

advised by my employers in London that we are to be met
by a representative of the British Embassy, a senior Greek
police officer . . . and a certain Chief Superintendent Delphick of Scotland Yard.''

"Splendid! Sound man, Delphick. I made it clear that
they should send him. When I rang a friend of ours in
London from that little bar. D'you know, Macallister, I'm
sure that blighter of a waiter overcharged me!''

"All right, all right. So I underestimated the extent of
your influence. All the same, before we arrive I must insist
on knowing the exact official status of Miss Emily Seeton.
I presume she is the person you keep dropping hints about.''

"Ah, well, I'm not too sure—''

"Enough, now!'' Macallister picked up the telephone on
the desk in his day cabin and pressed one of several buttons
on its base. "Purser? Captain here. My compliments to Miss
Emily Seeton, and I'd be obliged if she could spare me a
few moments of her time. Yes. Escort her here as soon as
possible.'' A cold grey Caledonian eye was again fixed on
Colveden. "Now, sir. Is the lady attached to the Metropolitan Police or is she not?''

"Straight question, that. I like a man who asks a straight
question—''

"And I'd like you the better if you'd stop havering and
give me a straight answer.''

"Oh, very well, then. Yes. Miss Seeton is officially retained by the Metropolitan Police.''

"As what, for heaven's sake? I've made it my business
to take a wee look at her. She looks too meek and mild
even to ask a policeman to help her across the street.''

"Take it from me, old boy, she doesn't need any help
crossing the street. Officially, Miss Seeton is a police artist.
She was an art teacher before she retired. Unofficially, Miss
Seeton has been responsible for putting more bad 'uns behind bars than you've had hot dinners. Well, no. To be

absolutely honest it couldn't amount to anything like as many as that. You're about forty-five, I'd say, and assuming at least three hundred hot dinners a year—''

Mercifully, the telephone rang at that moment and Captain Macallister was spared the conclusions to which Colveden's mental arithmetic was inexorably leading. ''Yes? She's *what?* Have you got the doctor to her? With her now? What's her cabin number? Right. I'm on my way.''

Sir George was already on his feet, concern written all over his ruddy, kindly face; and even Macallister was moved to confide in him. ''She wasn't anywhere to be seen, so the purser went to her cabin. She's been attacked, Colveden. Knocked out and damn nearly suffocated. But I'm told she's just coming round. Come on!''

''So foolish of me,'' Miss Seeton murmured feebly as the doctor gently sponged the contusion on the side of her head. ''No, thank you, Doctor, but I try to avoid taking pills of any kind . . . if I might perhaps have a cup of tea instead . . .'' She blinked as she looked up and noticed that the purser and the doctor had now been joined by the captain and Sir George. ''Oh, dear, I am sorry to be such a nuisance.''

At this point Sir George showed the sterling stuff of which he was made. ''Rubbish, m'dear,'' he huffed. ''All very concerned. Can't have this sort of thing going on, you know. Anyway, you don't want me blunderin' about in here. I'll go and fetch Meg. And organise that cup of tea.''

''So kind.''

With reluctant respect, Captain Macallister watched him go. Then he turned to the medical officer. ''Well, Doctor?''

''No bones broken, sir. Miss Seeton's had a severe shock, and she's going to have a nasty bump on her head for a few days, but the lady seems to be remarkably fit considering her—um, that is, remarkably fit.''

"Hospital treatment necessary? Should we arrange for an ambulance to be at the quayside?"

"Unnecessary in my view, sir."

"Glad to hear it. Miss Seeton, we shall soon arrive at Piraeus. I understand that a colleague of yours from London will be there to meet the ship, and if you feel well enough by then you'll no doubt want to talk to him. The purser and I will leave you now, but may I ask one quick question first?"

"Of course, Captain."

"Have you any idea who attacked you?"

"I didn't see the person, I'm afraid . . ."

And that was all Captain Macallister got out of Miss Seeton.

"Thank you for agreeing to this second discussion, Captain Macallister," Delphick said some three hours later. "My Greek colleague, Captain Papagiannis, is aware that we are meeting, but both he and the few English-speaking men he has available are extremely busy with other interviews, as you may well imagine. So he has kindly agreed that I may independently pursue points of particular interest to me. He and I will of course be comparing notes later. As you know, Miss Seeton is feeling much better now, so thank goodness we have only one murder to investigate, not two. I have had no more than a brief word with her so far, and hope to talk to her at greater length presently."

"The doctor tells me she's a tough old bird."

"She is indeed. Before I do see her again, I'd like to make sure that I have the sequence of events leading up to the attack on her right, if you don't mind. When we first came aboard, you explained to Papagiannis and me that you requested all the passengers to assemble in the lounge at nine-thirty, and you went there and spoke to them. That's correct, isn't it?"

"Aye."

"To let them know officially that Adrian Witley was dead, and that you had received new instructions to sail here direct. About how long did that meeting last?"

Macallister made a peculiarly Scottish noise in his throat before replying. "Perhaps fifteen minutes. Would have been longer if that auld—beg your pardon, if Sir George Colveden hadnae—"

"Quite. Miss Seeton was of course present at that meeting."

"Aye. She was sitting near tae Lady Colveden."

"Captain Macallister. Please look at the names on this list. Do you happen to remember if any or all of these people were in the lounge just before you and your officers left, when Sir George made what he persuaded himself to be a veiled reference to Miss Seeton?"

Macallister took the sheet of paper Delphick handed to him and studied it. Several times his eyebrows rose and fell slightly, but he made no comment while reading. When he eventually handed the paper back it was with a slight shake of the head.

"I canna really say. Ye'll appreciate that although I try tae meet every passenger at least once during a cruise, it's too much tae remember all their names. Sir Wormelow Tump I know, of course, he's one of the lecturers. He was there. So was the sleek wee man with the funny name. Zaybow. And Witley's lady friend, Blodwen Griffiths—d'ye mind my asking how ye set about making this list?"

Delphick smiled. "It may surprise you to learn that Sir George Colveden prepared it. And even more when I tell you that Tump and Szabo—that's pronounced 'Sabow' with an 'a' as in 'glass,' by the way—are both close friends of his."

"And he's accusing them of murder?"

"Good heavens, no. The thing about Colveden is that he

may often sound like a bit of a silly ass, but as a matter of fact he's a very shrewd old boy. And scrupulously fair-minded. After he heard that Witley had been murdered, he drew up an annotated list of all the people, not excluding his friends, he thought might conceivably have done away with him. He pushed it into my hand within a couple of minutes of my coming on board. I've shown you only the names. I'm keeping his comments to myself for the moment.''

"And what difference does it make whether they were at the meeting I called or not?''

"In the case of Tump and Szabo, none whatever. They know perfectly well who Miss Seeton is and the sort of work she has done for the Metropolitan Police during recent years. Most of the others on Colveden's list probably don't. Miss Seeton's attracted a fair amount of press attention in the past, but not on the part of the sort of newspapers your passengers are likely to read, and she's unknown outside Britain. Nevertheless, it occurred to me that if, as seems likely, Witley's murderer was there when Colveden blurted out that there was a Scotland Yard expert on board, he or she might have put two and two together and decided to lay in wait for Miss Seeton in her cabin.''

"To kill her, you mean? Silence her in case she'd already worked out who did it?''

"Perhaps. She's tough, as your medical officer noticed, and she keeps herself very fit by practising yoga. All the same, she does look like a caricature of a frail, elderly spinster. A person might act on the false assumption that one good knock on the head would finish her off. So you might be right, but I don't think so. I think somebody knew or found out that Miss Seeton's genius expresses itself in the drawings she makes, and went to search her cabin for what might turn out to be incriminating evidence.''

"A wee bit farfetched, I'd think, Mr. Delphick.''

Delphick shook his head. "I beg to differ. You see, so far as Miss Seeton can remember, all the conventional views she's sketched of the places you've visited are present and correct in the drawer where she keeps them. Between you and me, they're no more than competent, academic pieces of work, as she'd be the first to agree. It's the brilliantly imaginative drawings she makes of people that have all been stolen. I'm just hoping that we can either find them, or that Miss Seeton might be able to re-create them."

chapter
~ 14 ~

PHOTOGRAPHS HAD BEEN taken, and the fingerprint man and the other experts had gone away with their plastic envelopes and other impedimenta. Above all, the body of Adrian Witley had, to the huge relief of Captain Macallister and everybody else on board, at last been removed from the *Eurydice*. It had lain in his cabin for what both the ship's doctor and the Greek medical examiner agreed must have been something like twenty-four hours since he had been killed: it seemed much longer to those who had known about it soonest.

"Killed with a modern copy of a classical bust of Hercules. A curious choice of murder weapon, it seems to me," Captain Papagiannis suggested as he and Delphick sat together over a bottle of Glenmorangie single malt whisky. This had been sportingly provided by Captain Macallister, who had taken a dram with them. He then discreetly left them to their discussion, having satisfied himself that Delphick was educated enough to add just enough water to his glass to bring out the flavour and aroma of the whisky, and noting also that Papagiannis sensibly watched the pair of them and followed suit. Needless to say, ice had not been made available to his guests. The master of the *Eurydice* was not an unreasonable man, but there were certain practices he could not abide and would not tolerate when he played host.

"Oh, I don't know, except that it does seem to indicate that the murder was probably committed on impulse. The bust is quite heavy, but small enough to be gripped in one hand, and it was readily to hand. The steward confirmed that Witley must have brought it aboard in his luggage, because he'd noticed it on display in the cabin from the beginning of the cruise."

"Yes, I remember." Papagiannis took another sip of Glenmorangie and savoured it. Then he sighed. "It's good to have been able to send nearly all the passengers to their hotels, but . . ."

"But you're wondering if we've kept the right ones on board, Captain," Delphick said with a crooked little smile. Each man had copies of the passenger list and of a list of the names of all members of the crew. All of the latter were still on board the ship. Delphick supposed that they were none too pleased at having been denied shore leave, but that was just their bad luck.

Papagiannis picked up his copy of the passenger list. Beside each name a letter had been added in one of four different colours, to show the present whereabouts of that person. A, B, and C, in black, green, and blue respectively, signified the three hotels in Athens in which the vast majority were now accommodated. The remaining names stood out particularly, because they had been underlined in red, and the letter E, for *Eurydice*, placed beside them.

"Well, it is quite a short list, isn't it? 'Bookbinder, Dr. Dorcas'. She's the American, isn't she? 'Colveden, Sir George and Lady; Griffiths, Dr. Blodwen; Nash, Mr. Richard; Popjoy, Miss Juliana'—who shares a cabin with Mr. Nash, I see." Captain Papagiannis raised an amused eyebrow.

"Far from unusual in Britain these days," Delphick

pointed out, and Papagiannis nodded in man-to-man understanding.

"I do apologise for my tactlessness."

"No, no, my dear captain, I wasn't implying—"

"Of course not. 'Seeton, Miss Emily; Taylor, Mr. Frank'—"

"I should explain that that's the name on his passport," Delphick interjected. He was despairing of persuading this imaginative Greek that he and Mel Forby were not engaged in a torrid affair, or even a lukewarm one for that matter, but it was important that he should get the facts about the suspects right. "He's a naturalised British subject, but he's known professionally by his original name of Ferencz Szabo."

"Thank you. I had wondered about that. 'Tump, Sir Wormelow'—how fond you English are of your titles! And of course you and I, and your charming friend Miss Amelita Forby, will all be spending the night on board."

"Miss Seeton's friend, Captain. As I have mentioned previously. Several times."

"Yes, yes, of course. I see that you and she are to be accommodated in separate cabins."

It was subtly done, but Delphick could have sworn that Papagiannis winked conspiratorially as he leaned forward to reach for the Glenmorangie bottle. He decided that a combination of dignified silence on the subject of sleeping arrangements and a sober, businesslike approach to the matter in hand were the only possible tactics to adopt. Well, reasonably sober. The single malt whisky was remarkably good, and presumably Captain Macallister was able to obtain it duty free, so one need not feel too bad about the amount already gone from the bottle.

"Quite. All the other passengers have surrendered their passports and it will be easy enough to keep them under general supervision for the next day or two, longer if necessary. But I'm pretty sure our murderer is on board, Captain.''

''You have great faith in your Miss Seeton.''

''I do indeed, and with good reason. Nevertheless, it is essential for you and me jointly to interview everybody on the list, and form our own opinions. We need also to check their individual accounts of their movements on the day of the murder against each other.''

''I hate checking alibis,'' Papagiannis said with unexpected passion.

''So do I. But it often pays dividends. And I think it's no bad thing to wait until tomorrow morning to see these people. The innocent ones will be the more clearheaded after a good night's sleep, and the murderer will be that much more tense for having been left to stew. By the way, you have arranged for a man to be posted outside Miss Seeton's cabin, haven't you?''

''Of course. And for a relief to take over after every four hours. There will be no further attack upon Miss Seeton while my men are on duty, I promise you. So you and Miss Forby can look forward to an uninterrupted night's . . . sleep.''

''How does she seem to be feeling now, Doctor?'' Mel demanded the moment the door opened and the medical officer began to emerge from the cabin. It was her third attempt to visit Miss Seeton since she had come aboard in the company of Delphick immediately after the ship docked, and she very much hoped that this one would be successful. Having been waylaid by Sir George Colveden and treated to a long but characteristically disjointed account of the events of the past twenty-four hours, she arrived at Miss Seeton's cabin for the first time only to be ordered away by the stern and properly zealous Greek policeman who had been put on guard outside the door.

When she came back bearing a hastily scribbled note of authority from the ever-gallant Captain Papagiannis and was duly allowed to go inside, it was to find that Miss Seeton was so soundly asleep, a seraphic little smile on her face, that Mel hadn't the heart to disturb her. On this third occasion she had been told that the ship's doctor was with his patient, which sounded ominous.

"She's fine. As lively as a—"

"Miss Forb— that is, I mean, Mel? Is that really you?"

Mel smiled to hear the well-remembered voice again. "Yes. Hi! I just came to see how you are."

"Oh, do please come in, my dear! Whatever brings you all the way from England?"

"Why you, of course! Even though I didn't know until I got to Greece that you've been in the wars again."

"The wars? How absurd! Why, it was merely . . . dear, dear, I am forgetting my manners. I haven't introduced Marty Hussingtree, who has been so kind and attentive. He is really an actor, you know, but has been resting, such a silly expression, when Marty works so hard. He has Sir John Gielgud's autograph, and . . . Marty, this is my friend Amelita Forby, who—"

"Ooh! Mel Forby of the *Daily Negative*? In person? Lucky old me!" Merty whipped out his autograph book immediately and leafed through it, muttering to himself. Then he gazed in awe into Mel's eyes and offered her the book, with a ballpoint pen he produced from the breast pocket of his white tunic. "I haven't got any Fleet Street superstars yet, but if you wouldn't mind the page opposite David Frost . . . ?"

"Not at all," Mel said, scribbling away. "As long as it's okay by Frostie."

"How *super*, thanks ever so! I was just going to plump up Miss S's pillows for her, she lets me call her Miss S, you know, such a pet, isn't she, and when you think what she's been through!''

Mel looked on in amusement until the young man finally finished fussing, and wagged a roguish finger at Miss Seeton. "Now you ring that bell the *moment* you need anything, or I shall be quite cross with you, Miss S."

"Oh, dear, that would never do. But my usual cup of tea in the morning is all I could possibly want, thank you."

"All right, then. Nighty-night! Lovely to meet you, Miss Forby."

When the steward had finally ogled and squirmed his way out of the cabin, Mel sat down and surveyed Miss Seeton. "You're looking good," she said. "In spite of the ministrations of that weirdo."

"Marty means well, I'm sure. But I must admit that he can be a little exhausting."

"How are you, Miss Seeton? Really."

"Perfectly well, thank you. The bump on my head is still somewhat painful, but after the nap I had a little earlier, I hardly feel ready yet. To go to sleep again, that is. Especially as it still isn't quite ten o'clock. So I should have been feeling rather bored. Had you not come to talk to me, that is. Tell me, how is Mr. Banner?"

"He'd love it if you could bring yourself to call him Thrudd, you know. Even though it is an idiotic sort of name. Anyway, he's fine, thanks. We recently came back from holiday, which is why it was news to me until a few days ago that you were on this cruise."

A charming smile appeared on the pale little face looking up from the pillow. "I was so excited when Mr. Delphick telephoned me to say that I had won a merit award. Imagine, Mel, a merit award!"

"Yes. I heard about the, uh, merit award. Listen, Miss Seeton. Mind if I ask you a couple of questions? You aren't too sleepy?"

"Not a bit. I feel so wide awake that I expect I shall get up and make a few little sketches presently."

"Mr. Delphick will be very happy to hear that. The thing is, I want to be able to file a story for my paper first thing in the morning. All I sent my editor early this evening is what's gone out on the agency wires anyway: that the famous TV professor, Adrian Witley, died suddenly on board this ship yesterday. The holiday company hasn't released any details, but tomorrow you can bet your bottom dollar there'll be a flock of my rivals snooping around Athens and even trying to come aboard to question you."

"Oh, dear. But I know nothing about Mr. Witley's—"

"Maybe not. But somebody thinks you do or you wouldn't have been clobbered this morning. Look, Mr. Delphick knows I'm talking to you, and I'm honour bound to let him you tell him all you can about the murder first. So I'm not going to ask you about Witley. Can you tell me about two other people I've never met or heard of before, though? It might help me to make sense of anything Mr. Delphick feels he can pass on to me before all the world hears about it. First, this American, Dorcas Bookbinder."

"Dear Dorcas! Such a very clever person, I do admire her. She is a great expert on Carpaccio. The whole Venetian School, in fact. Not a subject one would expect to interest someone with such an austere religious . . . I have often thought it a little unfair that they should have rather monopolised the name. The puritans, that is."

"What name?"

"Why, Dorcas. The charitable woman of Joppa. In the Acts, you know. Of the Apostles. I am sure Mr. Delphick would know. And he might be able to explain about faith and works, which I have always found very confusing—"

"This Dr. Bookbinder is an art historian, then," Mel cut in ruthlessly. It was a choice between that and the sensation of wading through a pool of treacle that she often experi-

enced when in Miss Seeton's company. "What about Blodwen Griffiths?"

"Oh, there I do feel that Professor Witley was at fault.
He was of course naturally agitated after nearly falling off—
but should, I think, have accepted that Miss Griffiths
merely—the mountain path, I should have said. The edge.
That he nearly—"

"She's in the cruise brochure. Guest lecturer. Old coins."

"Numismatics is the technical term, I believe. I had been
so looking forward to her lecture, but of course the captain's
address to us all took priority, and then again poor Miss
Griffiths was so upset that she could hardly have, by Professor Witley's death, that is, been expected to be able to
concentrate on them. Early Greek coins, I mean."

"I guess not," Mel said thoughtfully, having for once
allowed Miss Seeton to finish one of her marathon sentences
in her own way. Like most popular journalists she was well
aware of the late Adrian Witley's reputation as a successful
womaniser, and was now groping towards a possible explanation of the continuing presence on board of eight of
the passengers. Well, only four of them, really. The ship's
doctor didn't want Miss Seeton moved for the present, and
Delphick would obviously have wanted to keep the Colvedens on hand. Also Szabo and Tump, who were in effect
honorary members of "the Plummergen gang."

That left three women and Dickie Nash, whom Delphick
must regard as suspects. Come to think of it, old Colveden
had started burbling something about women scorned, but
in all the hurly-burly it hadn't been possible to pay proper
attention. Hmm. Juliana Popjoy. Dorcas Bookbinder. Blodwen Griffiths. Must form an impression of each of them.
Also of course this Dickie Nash character, who was Popjoy's
man. Was he perhaps the possessive, jealous type? Had
Witley made a pass at Popjoy? A successful one? It was
easy enough to infer from Miss Seeton's rambling comments

that there had been something between Witley and Griffiths, but where did Bookbinder fit in?

It would be worth going to see if any of them were around in the bar. And then—now that a telephone line had been connected to the ship—perhaps a word or two with the reference librarian at the *Daily Negative*. Delphick was a professional detective, Miss Seeton—though she'd deny it, of course—a brilliant amateur. Still, there ought to be *something* an investigative reporter could do to help.

"Thanks, Miss Seeton. It's been great talking to you, and a relief to see that you're doing so well. Sleep well, now, and I'll see you in the morning. Good night."

"Good night, Miss, er, Mel."

chapter
~15~

AFTER LEAVING MISS Seeton, Mel went to the purser's office. There, thanks to a fairly simple exercise of her feminine wiles, she persuaded the telephonist on duty to allow her the use of a tiny but soundproof cubicle for a lengthy call to the duty reference librarian at the offices of the *Daily Negative* in London. After that, she made her way to the main lounge.

The bar was open, but the steward in charge of it wasn't rushed off his feet. Mel had supposed that the few passengers left on board the *Eurydice* would have gathered together for mutual comfort and support, but she had underestimated the effects of fear and suspicion. The seven people in the room were in fact well spread out, and gave no impression of looking for company. Indeed it struck Mel that they looked as if they were maintaining some sort of surveillance over one another.

Dorcas Bookbinder was sitting alone, pretending to read a book. Dickie Nash and Juliana Popjoy were together in a corner, quietly conversing. Even the ebullient Sir George Colveden seemed subdued as he sat with his wife. Wormelow Tump and Ferencz Szabo were on their feet near the bar, more or less in conversation but not looking as if their hearts were in it. There was no sign of Blodwen Griffiths, who had presumably taken refuge in her cabin.

Everybody looked in her direction when Mel entered the room, and both Colvedens smiled at her, Meg giving her a little wave. Mel was tempted to join them, but then decided that it would be more productive for her to try to become acquainted with the three unknown quantities, so she simply beamed at her friends and then marched boldly over to Dickie Nash and Juliana Popjoy. Both these sophisticates knew how to behave, and Nash was on his feet by the time Mel reached them.

"Hello. I'm Amelita Forby, we met very briefly earlier on. Do you mind if I join you?"

"Delighted," Nash said. "Juliana and I were just agreeing that you must be feeling you've come aboard a latter-day version of the *Marie Celeste*. Do sit down. May I get you a drink? We need refills ourselves."

"Thanks. A gin and tonic would be nice." Juliana made room for Mel on the sofa and patted the seat invitingly while Dickie pottered to the bar, taking his and Juliana's empty glasses with him.

"The *Marie Celeste* was deserted, I know," Juliana said. "And we're here. But we must seem like a collection of ghosts."

Mel grinned. "Oh, hardly that. Ghosts don't smell deliciously of Penhaligon scent." She forbore to add that, even though clearly under strain, Juliana was one of the most exuberantly flesh-and-blood people she'd met for many a long day.

"You recognize it! How clever of you. One of the pleasures of living in Bath is that Penhaligon's have a branch there."

"I used to be a fashion reporter. It was my job to know what smart ladies wear besides clothes." Dickie wandered back in the company of the bar steward with their drinks on a tray, and Mel smiled her thanks as she raised her glass. "Thank you. Cheers."

Dickie sighed as he lowered himself back into his armchair facing the two women on the sofa. "Cheers indeed. Let's hope so, anyway. Thank goodness you showed up, Miss Forby."

"Please call me Mel. The Amelita bit's strictly for byline purposes. Actually, I was christened Amelia. I ask you, do I look like an Amelia?"

Dickie surveyed her judiciously from head to toe, and Mel shuddered involuntarily. It wasn't that she found him attractive, but she was nevertheless very conscious of being in the presence of a man with a strong sexual drive. A man capable, perhaps, of being consumed with murderous jealousy if a potential rival for the affections of the voluptuous woman at her side were to appear on the scene.

"No, I can't say you do. Mind you, I'm prejudiced. When I was a child my nanny was called Amelia, and you certainly don't resemble her in any way."

"Good, that's settled, then. But I can't think why you're pleased to see me. Most cultivated people regard journalists from the popular press as being uncivilized yahoos."

Juliana made a pleasant little noise, halfway between a chuckle and a gurgle. "That's it, Mel, the best form of defence is attack. Actually, I rather think Dickie's relieved to be able to talk to somebody he knows for sure isn't a murderer. You could cut the atmosphere in here with a knife. Incidentally, your Fleet Street rivals must be green with envy."

"About what?"

"Your relationship with that very important and rather scary but at the same time reassuring Scotland Yard detective."

"My . . . ? Oh, for heaven's sake, there's nothing between me and Mr. Delphick!" In the following few seconds nothing was said, but Mel saw the conspiratorial look that passed between the other two, and realised that she could deny the charge till she was blue in the face without doing the slightest good.

It was a disconcerting feeling. For crying out loud, she didn't even know Delphick's first name! It was flattering in a way, of course, to be assumed to be his mistress. Delphick was undeniably an impressive man, even a bit of a charmer in his way, and if she had been the sort of girl who went for older men, he . . . well, never mind that. You'd think a person just back from a happy, sensual holiday in the company of her lover ought to be ready for a quiet life. Instead of being so erotically turned on as she seemed to be these days.

For the first time since she had been acquainted with him, Mel found herself wondering what it would be like to go to bed with Chief Superintendent Delphick, and once in her consciousness the notion proved to be both unexpectedly attractive and difficult to dislodge. She shuddered again, this time rather pleasurably, and tried to concentrate on the matter in hand, which was to decide whether or not either Juliana Popjoy or Dickie Nash could have murdered Adrian Witley and thereafter attacked Miss Seeton.

"Anyway, at least you've got each other to talk to," Mel pressed on rather lamely. "I mean, surely you don't suspect each other?"

"Good lord, no," Dickie said at once. Was that the slightest hint of uncertainty in his voice? Mel noticed that Juliana didn't reply, and that there was an enigmatic little smile on her face.

"Mind you," Dickie went on, "we're not looking forward to being subjected to the third degree by your gentleman friend. By the way, this conversation is, what's the phrase, off the record, isn't it?"

"Of course."

"Yes. Good. You see . . . oh, Lord, I don't know . . . never mind. Forget it." He waved a hand in embarrassment and silence fell again until Juliana came to his rescue.

"The thing is, Mel, that Dickie and I are in a slightly awkward position and could do with some strictly confidential advice. I'm so glad you came over to talk to us. We were planning to seek you out, to sound you out about the line we should take when it's our turn to be interviewed. You see, neither of us really thinks for a moment that the other one had anything to do with this, this murder, but either of us *could* have done it, I suppose, without the other knowing. Depending on when it happened. And we each had what some people might think was a motive."

Mel goggled at her. "You *each* did?"

"Yes. A few months ago Adrian Witley was responsible for my losing a great deal of money—"

"Be fair, my love," Dickie cut in. "Strictly speaking, he was responsible for your not making a huge windfall profit."

"Yes. All right. But a huge windfall profit—a small fortune in fact—that I strongly suspect Witley eventually shared with Crivelli."

"Sorry, who's Crivelli?" Mel enquired.

"An Italian collector," Dickie said. "He's one of the passengers too, but they let him go to a hotel in Athens. We're fairly sure they were in cahoots, even though he and Witley were pretending not to know each other before, er, it happened."

Juliana went on. "I was absolutely furious when I found out, of course. And I must admit that if Adrian Witley had walked into my shop again a week later, I'd cheerfully have brained him myself. I can't even begin to pretend I'm not glad that somebody seems to have done it for me. I was livid not only because he deliberately deceived me and set me up, but because that money would have been a godsend. The fact is, Dickie and I are—''

"In a bit of a financial mess, frankly. At least, I am. Was, I mean.'' The personal magnetism he had been giving out earlier seemed to have faded, and Nash looked old, tired and disillusioned, fed up with the world and with himself.

"I'm a gambler, I'm afraid,'' he went on. "Compulsive. How Juliana puts up with me I really don't know. Sometimes I win, but lately I've been on a dreadful losing streak. Fact is, a few months ago I was in such a hole that I borrowed a hell of a lot of money. From Witley, of all people. Idiot that I am. Though in my own defence I should explain that this was before Juliana and I found out about the deception he'd practised on her at the shop.'' He seemed to lose control of his voice for a moment, and paused for several seconds before continuing.

"Well, to cut a long story short, Witley not unnaturally started pressing me to pay him back. More or less politely at first, then nastily. Very nastily indeed, culminating in . . . culminating in, well, I call it blackmail. He offered me— us—two alternatives. Either he'd make a scandal at Cambridge and get me booted out of my Fellowship. Or— or . . .''

Mel was astonished to see a tear trickle down his cheek. He fumbled for a handkerchief while Juliana spoke for him.

"Or I was to make myself available to him at any time he chose. And not only that. With at least a show of enthusiasm.''

"What a *bastard*!''

"Thank you for saying that, Mel. Dickie wasn't at all sure it would be wise to confide in you, but now I know we were right to.''

"But whatever possessed you to come on this cruise?''

Juliana shrugged. "We argued endlessly about it. I would do anything—yes, pretty well *anything*—for Dickie. I know you shouldn't give in to blackmail, but I was so desperate I might have done what the beastly man wanted. Actually, I think I'd have tried to appeal to his better nature, if . . . or maybe . . . God, I shall never know now, I suppose. Maybe push him overboard.''

"I don't see how anybody could have blamed you if you had,'' Mel said. "But how on earth can I help you?''

"By interceding for us with your friend, perhaps. It must be as obvious to you as it is to us that we're suspects. You know this Mr. Delphick. Do you think that if we come absolutely clean with him, and assuming he finds out who did it, he'd try to keep this sordid side of it quiet?''

"I'm absolutely certain of it,'' Mel said at once.

"And . . . and—listen, Mel, Dickie and I aren't famous at all. You are. The moment we heard your name we knew that sooner or later you'd find out all our grubby little secrets. But we're just a couple of ordinary people, and . . . well, sorry to say this, but the tabloid papers do go in for—''

"Invading people's privacy for the sake of a bit of scandal? You're right, of course, but it's not my style. Dickie, I told you this conversation's off the record, and I meant it. Let me explain something to you. The only reason I'm here is because Miss Seeton's mixed up in all this. I'll admit I feel distinctly proprietorial about her. My experience tells me that between them, she and Delphick will work out who killed Adrian Witley, and that's the exclusive story I'm after. If the murderer does turn out to be one of you, tough luck. But—sorry, Dickie, I was about to say I'd bet my bottom dollar it won't.'' Mel stood up.

"On the assumption you'll end up in the clear, I wouldn't dream of betraying your confidence—except to Delphick, if you really want me to give him the gist of this before he talks to you.''

Juliana and Dickie both nodded. "We do. And thank you, Mel."

"Fine. See you in the morning. Try not to worry too much. At least you're out of the frying pan, and I have a feeling the fire's reserved for somebody else."

Having told the *Negative*'s librarian that she would call her back in half an hour or so, Mel decided to postpone any attempt to get into conversation with Dorcas Bookbinder. In any case, her talk to Juliana and Dickie had left her with quite enough to think about for the time being.

She therefore returned to the telephone, made good her promise, and listened intently, scribbling a few notes as she learned what the *Negative*'s "morgue," *Who's Who*, and the other basic reference books to hand had yielded to a skilled researcher. Confirmation of the most interesting item of information couldn't be obtained until after ten the next morning British time, but it was nevertheless in a very positive frame of mind that Mel went to find out if Delphick had finished his conference with his Greek colleague and gone to his own cabin as he had told her he planned to do.

Mel knew the number and soon found her way to the appropriate corridor. It was important, she told herself, for Delphick to know as soon as possible both what she had been told by Juliana Popjoy and Dickie Nash, and what she had gleaned from her colleague in London. There was no need whatever for her to feel nervous about disturbing him late in the evening. Delphick was on board the *Eurydice* in order to investigate a murder—with a putatively murderous assault on Miss Seeton thrown in for good measure. It was imperative that any information that seemed likely to advance that investigation should be communicated to him at once, however late it was.

Yes, but that being so, why was her throat unaccountably dry and her heart pounding like the proverbial steam hammer? And why, if it came to that, had she stopped off in a ladies' room on the way and renewed her lipstick? For goodness *sake*, Forby, Mel asked herself sternly, what is the matter with you? You are a seasoned Fleet Street hack, not an impressionable teenager in search of holiday romance! Get on with it, woman!

Several deep breaths did nothing either for her heartbeat or the dryness in her throat, but they did make Mel Forby look adorably flustered when Delphick, himself in a state of euphoria induced by Macallister's Glenmorangie, answered her tap on his door. It seemed the most natural thing in the world to greet her with a hug and a big kiss.

A kiss returned with such enthusiasm that the one thing, as they say, led to another.

chapter
~16~

BY THE TIME Delphick woke up, Mel had departed from his cabin. He lay there in a daze for a few minutes, wondering first where he was. Then, having remembered that he was on board the *Eurydice*, he tried for a little while to persuade himself that what he had experienced was an unusually vivid and delightful dream. The hint of perfume that lingered about the bedclothes soon obliged him to accept that it had been no dream, and he sat bolt upright, shocked. What on earth had happened to his judgment, his self-control, his sense of responsibility? A skinful of malt whisky followed by an abandoned bout of lovemaking with a woman young enough to be his daughter must result in terrible retribution. In immediate physical terms, a ghastly hangover. Then, an awful burden of guilt and mortification lasting who could say how long? For the rest of his life, perhaps.

Groaning experimentally, he swung his legs out and sat on the side of the bed. He blinked a few times. How very odd. No hangover. His mouth was dry and tasted disagreeable, but his head was crystal-clear. There seemed little point in going on groaning, so he stopped, and went over to the washbasin where he cleaned his teeth. Better and better, physically at least: he had escaped a hangover. The guilt and shame were no doubt lurking in the background, waiting either to pounce and overwhelm him, or to insinuate themselves into his mind and spirit, working like a slow poison. Well, a man might as well brace himself with a refreshing hot shower in the meantime.

While under the shower, the recollection of certain delicious details of what had transpired after that first astonishing kiss surged unbidden into Delphick's consciousness, and he realised with another shock that so far he didn't regret a thing, and rather doubted if in the foreseeable future he was going to. On the contrary, he felt proud, honoured, elated, and about twenty years younger. As a matter of fact, he decided as he towelled himself off, he felt marvellous, and for the first time in years burst into song while he dressed. He couldn't remember many of the words that followed "It's a Hap-Hap-Happy Day," but "toodle-oodle-oodle ay" filled in the gaps perfectly satisfactorily, and he saw no reason to desist when he left the cabin and walked springily along the corridor, skipping a few steps now and then to work off some of the extraordinary surplus of energy he seemed to have available.

Delphick looked at his watch as he entered the dining salon. It was seven forty-five, he could eat a horse, and—splendid! Miss Seeton was up and very much about, already helping herself at the buffet. The bruising from the blow she had received on the side of her head extended colorfully well below the hairline, but the doctor had evidently decided that it was unnecessary for her to continue to wear a dressing.

"*Good* morning, Miss Seeton!" he carolled from the doorway before hastening over to her side. "And how do *you* feel today?"

"Why, good morning, Mr. Delphick. Oh, a great deal better, thank you so much. And how well *you* look!"

"Do I? If this ship were going somewhere, I'd attribute

it to the sea air. As it is, let me be gallant and say it's because I'm very pleased to see you on your feet. You're up early."

"Do you know, that is what my cabin steward said. He seemed quite upset when he arrived with a cup of tea for me. Because I was already up, that is. Having spent so long in bed yesterday, I was quite wakeful. During the night, I mean. So I heard. I wonder who it could have been?"

Delphick observed that Miss Seeton had already made her breakfast selection, and hastily loaded a plate for himself. "Shall we go and sit down over there?"

Settled at the table, he could hardly wait to start eating, but the question had to be asked. With any luck Miss Seeton would take some time to get round to answering it, while he tucked a few mouthfuls away. "Who could what—I mean who—have been?"

"I beg your pardon?"

"During the night. Did somebody disturb you?"

"Somebody did try. Try the door. Twice, I think. It might have been the Greek policeman, I suppose. But he was the one who had urged me to bolt it. The door, from inside. In dumb show, of course. Such a charming young man, and so proud of his little son. We had no language in common, but he showed me some photographs he had with him. He had a packet of food that interested me. Not at all like our sandwiches. He was about five or six years old, I suppose. The little boy, that is. With his father's ears."

Having wolfed down most of the contents of his plate and drunk a cup of coffee, Delphick had stilled the worst of his hunger pangs and was ready to play his part. "The little boy in the photograph had his father's ears and a packet of interesting food?"

"No, no, the policeman. I had been worried about his being on duty outside my door for hours on end, you see, and he showed me his food. But nothing to drink. Perhaps

he had a flask of coffee or something hidden away somewhere. Oh, how nice, Mr. Delphick, here comes Miss
Forby!''

It was the moment of truth. As Mel approached, Delphick
did his best to look friendly in an official sort of way. ''Good
morning, Mel,'' he said, but was unable to prevent a broad
smile of pure delight from spreading over his face when he
saw the sparkling good humour in hers, and registered the
almost-imperceptible wink she directed at him.

''Good morning, Miss Seeton,'' Mel said demurely.
''Good to see you up here. And good morning to you, Mr.
Delphick. I'll just go and get some food and then join you,
if I may. I'm furiously hungry, for some reason.''

''You know, I believe I'd like some more myself. May
I bring you something, Miss Seeton?''

''Thank you, Mr. Delphick, but no. I hope to persuade
Dr. Bookbinder to run through some yoga exercises with
me a little later, so I mustn't eat too much.''

''Will you excuse us for a moment, then?''

Miss Seeton smiled happily and nodded, but gently, for
her bump was still very tender. At the buffet, Mel edged
close to Delphick.

''This is supposed to be an embarrassing moment,'' she
murmured, ''but since you look as happy as I feel, who
cares? I assume you got some sleep. How are you this
morning, you lovely man?''

''I'm walking on air,'' Delphick said simply. ''And I
don't mind if that is a cliché.''

''Wow! There's hope for you yet. I wanted to leave a
note for you, but I was afraid you might despise me for a
forward hussy. Now we must go back to the table and be
very good.''

''I'll try to keep my hands off you, dear Mel. But it isn't
going to be easy.''

• • •

"I'm glad we all decided to come to breakfast at the same time," Mel said, all brisk efficiency when they rejoined Miss Seeton. "Actually, I had a bit of news I should have passed on to you yesterday evening, Mr. Delphick. But then I found out you'd gone to your cabin, and something else came up, and it slipped my mind. It'll be of interest to you too, Miss Seeton, especially if you plan to be with Dorcas Bookbinder later. So I'll tell you both if I may."

"News?"

"Well, no. Information, actually, and already in the public domain, as they say. I was on the phone to my office yesterday evening, twice. The first time was to ask them to dig out anything whatever they could lay their hands on concerning Adrian Witley. Then I called back after they'd had a little time to dig around. As usual, good old *Who's Who* turned up trumps right away. Nearly all the full professors at the older universities are in it. Adrian Witley was once married. To one Dorcas Amy Bookbinder, of New Hampshire, USA. The marriage was dissolved two years ago. It had lasted three years, no children."

"Yes, of course," Miss Seeton murmured thoughtfully. "That would account for it."

"For what, Miss Seeton?"

"Well, you see, poor Dorcas was so nervous about seeing him again at the welcome party in Venice. With, er, a new lady friend."

Delphick whipped out his list of suspects and glanced at it. "That would be Blodwen Griffiths, I take it."

Mel nodded. "Right. Within a few hours my office should have a copy of the divorce certificate. The old rules were in force two years ago. Assuming it was Dorcas who sued for divorce, the certificate will show the name of the co-respondent. It's unlikely to be Blodwen, I should think. I'm told that according to the press cuttings that started accumulating about Witley as soon as he shot to television stardom, the gossip columnists have reported him as 'squiring'—their word, Mr. Delphick—any number of women."

Delphick sighed. "Well, Miss Seeton, you know and obviously like the former Mrs. Witley. I take it you wouldn't propose to run through yoga exercises with her if you thought she'd hit him on the head with a statuette of Hercules. Not to mention having a go at you, assuming that the same person was responsible."

Miss Seeton shook her head solemnly. "Oh, no. Dorcas is an expert on Carpaccio, you see. Will you please excuse me now?"

Mel and Delphick had been gazing at her, waiting for further enlightenment, but Miss Seeton gathered up her things with the serene air of one who has brought a long and complex chain of reasoning to an irrefutable conclusion, and began to rise. Delphick hastily leapt to his feet and drew her chair back for her. Miss Seeton smiled her thanks and then checked herself.

"Oh, dear, I almost forgot," she said, and took a sheaf of loose sheets from the top of the block of drawing paper in her capacious holdall. "These are only scribbles, I fear, but I have tried to reproduce the ones that somebody took from the bureau in my cabin. And there are two or three new ones I did last night. In view of your great kindness in arranging the merit award, I think I should hand them to you, Mr. Delphick."

Then Miss Seeton was gone, leaving Delphick torn between the desire to fall upon the drawings and a longing to talk quietly to Mel. Captain Papagiannis entered the dining salon, spotted them, and frustrated both alternatives.

"Ha! There you are. I thought I should find you together." He beamed from one to the other and nodded, well pleased with what he saw. "So you passed a happy night," he announced. "Good. Because now we have work to do,

Chief Superintendent. You will excuse us, dear Miss Forby? I will restore him to you as soon as possible.''

"There's no point in my beating about the bush, Mr., er, would you prefer me to call you Szabo or Taylor?'' Delphick asked fifteen minutes later, in the privacy of a spacious deluxe suite vacated by two of the wealthier passengers, a married German couple presently fretting in Athens. Delphick was seated at a writing table, with Miss Seeton's sketches tantalisingly on its surface but still uninspected, for Papagiannis had monopolised his attention since they left the dining salon.

"Taylor. It's my legal name.''

Delphick nodded. "Fine. You'll understand that this is an unorthodox sort of investigation, and to be quite candid, neither Captain Papagiannis nor I are entirely sure what sort of rules we should apply. So let me stress that if you agree to answer a few questions it must be of your own free will, and that nothing will be written down or used in evidence, no matter what.''

There was an enigmatic smile on Szabo's face. "No matter what,'' he repeated slowly. "You mean that if you eventually decide I murdered Witley, you'll begin all over again.''

"That's absolutely right. My Greek colleague and I merely want to try to clear the ground a bit, and an unbuttoned, off-the-record conversation might be helpful.'' Captain Papagiannis, who was all but submerged in a huge armchair in the corner, nodded his agreement. He had already had a brief chat with the dandified little man and had taken to him.

"We at Scotland Yard have good reason to be grateful to you for your past help,'' Delphick continued, "and if I'm prejudiced at all it's in your favour. Incidentally, you didn't kill Witley, I presume?''

"No. Quite the reverse, as a matter of fact. Witley tried to kill me. Once for certain, possibly twice."

"We'll come to that in a moment. Let's just examine the reasons you might have had for killing him. It's pretty much an open secret among people who interest themselves in these things in London that Witley was threatening you with an action for defamation of character."

"It was more of a Mexican standoff really. I was threatening him with the same."

"If it had come to the point, who do you think would have won?"

"I would. No question about it."

"How can you be so sure? You're a well-respected Mayfair dealer and therefore we can take it for granted you know your business. But you've never so far as I know claimed to be a scholar, or even an authority on any particular field."

"No, I haven't. I started by buying and selling army surplus stores, then moved on to dealing in Chelsea junk and a few decent antiques before I got my sights on Bond Street." Szabo grinned widely, proud of his achievements. "Which is why academic credentials cut no ice with me, and I know a fake when I see one."

"All right, but wasn't it a bit rash to pick on an eminent international authority on Greek antiquities to tangle with?"

"Somebody had to do it. Look, chum, we're not talking about your average crooked antique dealer putting a few wormholes in an old chair and flogging it to some innocent as Chippendale. Witley was operating in the big league. A genuine expert, yes, so people were naturally inclined to accept what he said. But Professor Adrian Witley was an audacious crook and a disgrace to his university. I'm quite sorry he's dead, in a way. I was looking forward quite a lot to blowing him out of the water in court."

"So it wasn't just a row about the bust Sotheby's was going to auction? You reckon you could have proved that this wasn't the first time he'd supplied false attributions so as to pass off fakes, do you?''

"Certainly, and I'm sure Witley knew it. The main reason I came on this cruise was to try to identify some of his contacts.''

"Well, from that point of view you've wasted your money, haven't you?''

"Oh, I wouldn't say that. Witley's dead so I won't be suing him, obviously. But I've identified another party who probably needs to be blacklisted by all reputable dealers and auction houses.''

"Here in Greece?''

"Well, I suppose you could put it like that. Look, I don't know if the forensic chaps or whoever are responsible can pinpoint the time of Witley's death, but a number of people can vouch for the fact that I went ashore at both the places we stopped at on—good heavens, was it really only the day before yesterday? The thing is, you need to . . . Delphick? Are you listening to a word I'm saying?'' Szabo paused, and then his chest swelled as he sucked in air. *"Wake up, you 'orrible man!''* he then bellowed, and smiled sweetly when both Delphick and Papagiannis started violently.

"There. You did say you wished you'd heard my sergeant-major imitation. Now may I have your attention, please?''

"My apologies, Mr. Taylor. I *was* listening, but then my eye happened to fall on—look, this other chap, the associate of Witley's you think might not be kosher. Is he a passenger on this ship?''

"In a manner of speaking, but he's not on board.''

"Ah.'' Delphick masked the greater part of Miss Seeton's variation on Lotto's portrait of Andrea Odoni, and held it out for Szabo to see. "Tell me, does he look like this?''

"Amazingly so. One of Miss Seeton's efforts, I presume.''

"Mind telling us his name? Oh, and would you please keep all this strictly to yourself for the present?"

"It's Carlo Crivelli. And you can trust me."

"I know that. Thank you. We may well need your help again later, but Captain Papagiannis and I need to get moving on something rather urgently. Do you mind?"

chapter
~17~

BLODWEN GRIFFITHS EVENTUALLY emerged from her seclusion shortly before ten that morning; too late for breakfast in the normal way of things. However, she was able to take advantage of the general listlessness that characterised the ship's regular routine in the absence of all but a handful of the passengers, and find a sufficiency of bits and pieces remaining on the buffet table.

She was, of course, observed. Sir George and Lady Colveden had been breakfasting late, and Juliana Popjoy and Dickie Nash were also there, lingering over their coffee at a distant table.

"George, I'm going to go over and ask that poor girl to join us," Meg said. "She must be desperately lonely and unhappy, and she hasn't even got Mrs. Golightly to talk to now."

"Absolutely. Good idea. Try and take her mind off things, eh?"

"Now you're not to bully her, dear."

Sir George was outraged. "*Me?* Bully a young woman? Good gracious, the very idea! Not my style at all!"

Meg patted his hand apologetically. "No, I know it isn't. I'm sorry, I didn't mean that really. But you can be the tiniest bit tactless sometimes, and I don't think you should ask her any questions. Especially now that Mr. Delphick's in charge.''

By the time his wife returned to their table with Dr. Blodwen Griffiths in tow, Sir George had got over his sense of affront, and rose to greet her. "Ah, jolly good. How d'ye do. Colveden's the name. Take a pew. Feeling a bit better, are you?''

Blodwen undoubtedly looked a great deal better than when last observed twenty-four hours earlier, during the meeting Captain Macallister had addressed. Her eyes were no longer puffy, her nose no longer red, and she had applied makeup to her face. She was smartly dressed, and the very picture of a thoroughly personable academic lady.

"Good morning, Sir George," she said composedly.

"Ah, the lilt of the valleys!" he exclaimed admiringly. "*Sospan bach* and all that. I had a battalion of Welsh Guards under my command once—"

"George? I don't think that Dr. Griffiths—"

"I'm sorry to disappoint you," the newcomer said at the same moment, "but I was born in Stoke Poges, just outside London. I have visited Wales once or twice, but only as a tourist. I'm afraid my Welsh name misled you." Blodwen Griffiths spoke with an impeccable Oxford accent, and after gaping at her for a moment Sir George admitted defeat, after his own fashion.

"There you are, you see, that just proves it doesn't do to go jumping to conclusions. What I always say is, people hear what they want to hear. I've noticed it time and time again. Stoke Poges, eh? Well, well."

"I understand there are only a few of us left on board. Are you suspects too?" Dr. Griffiths enquired pleasantly. Her manner was that of a fellow guest casually encountered at a cocktail party, making polite conversation. Even the normally self-contained Meg Colveden was startled.

"Well, I hardly know how to—"

"Forgive my asking, but before the Golightlys went ashore they told me there was a lot of speculation among the passengers about who was staying behind and why. Sweet people, they tried so hard to avoid the obvious implication in my own case."

Sir George harrumphed. "Now dash it all, haven't I just been saying people shouldn't jump to conclusions . . . ?"

"Oh, I entirely agree, but that's not at all the same thing as working something out logically, is it? I mean, everybody knows I was having an affair with Adrian. And most of you saw him humiliate me outside that monastery. It's perfectly obvious that if anybody had a reason to bash him over the head, B. Griffiths did."

"I say, how d'you know he was bashed over the head?" Sir George asked, his voice heavy with meaning.

"There you are, that's just what I mean. Actually, I found out from that gay steward. Men like that are born gossips."

"Well, if you are a murder suspect, I must say you sound quite cheerful about it," Meg pointed out. "You looked absolutely awful this time yesterday."

"Yes, I know. It hadn't really sunk in, I suppose. But now I've had a day and a night to think things over, face the situation honestly, and straighten myself out. The scales have fallen from my eyes, as they say. I realise what a stupid idiot I've been. A reasonably intelligent adult person allowing herself to be treated like a doormat, simply because . . . well, never mind about that. The important thing is that I'm free of him now, and it's time to try to recover my self-respect."

"Good for you, m'dear," Sir George said heartily, looking as if he was just managing to resist the temptation to slap her on the back.

"All the same," Blodwen continued, "I realise I've got to convince this man from Scotland Yard that it wasn't me. It's a good thing there are plenty of other suspects."

"You reckon so?"

"I know so. There's Dorcas, for a start. I don't know the exact terms she accepted at the time of the divorce settlement, but I should think—"

"Hang on a minute. D'you mean to say that charmin' American gel used to be married to Witley?"

"Yes indeed."

"Good heavens. And Miss Seeton says she's so clever."

"And I should think she stands to collect a fair amount in insurance money. I've always understood that the first thing detectives ask themselves in these situations is *cui bono?*"

"By jove, she's right, Meg! It's Latin, for 'who stands to benefit?' It's in my magistrates' manual somewhere or other."

"I know what *cui bono* means, George. Actually, it's 'to whom the benefit,' strictly speaking."

Blodwen lowered her voice. "Then there's Dickie Nash over there. I happen to know that he owed Adrian rather a lot of money, and couldn't pay it back. I'm not sure exactly how Adrian was pressuring Dickie, but knowing him, I'd say it would have been in a peculiarly nasty way. Dickie might not look it, but he's a proud man, and driven to it he could . . . well."

Meg intervened. "Excuse me, Blodwen—you don't mind if I call you Blodwen? Thank you. May I ask if you propose to tell Chief Superintendent Delphick all this?"

"Oh, no. At least, not if I can help it. I suppose it isn't a very ladylike thing to say, but I'm coming round to the idea that whoever did for Adrian is by way of being a public benefactor. I do hope it doesn't turn out to be that nice Ferencz Szabo. He must know that when it came to the point Adrian wouldn't have dared to take that business of the bust of Homer to court."

The Colvedens had both been reduced to silence by Blodwen Griffiths, and simply goggled at her as she went on in the same matter-of-fact way. "That leaves Wormelow Tump and you two, and try as I might I can't think why you're still here. Dear old Tump's gay too, of course, but unless Adrian was blackmailing him—"

"Sir Wormelow Tump is a good personal friend of mine, young lady." Sir George had recovered the power of speech and bristled at her. "He also happens to be a very distinguished member of Her Majesty's Household." Then, fair-minded as always, he shrugged. "Mind you, I'm not exactly denying, um, that is, I've often wondered . . . but take it from me, I've met a lot of thoroughly good eggs in my time that I wouldn't necessarily have volunteered to share a billet with. Remember the colonel at Aldershot I told you about years ago, Meg? Used to wear a silk frock and high-heeled shoes in the mess of an evening, and liked the chaps to call him Cynthia? Not on guest nights, needless to say."

"How utterly riveting," Blodwen said, her eyes wide. "Didn't the commanding officer mind?"

"Well, actually, he was the commanding officer. Anyway, that's beside the point. You're barking up the wrong tree so far as my friend Tump's concerned. He's here for the same reason Meg and I are." Sir George preened himself. "We have been able to render some service to Chief Superintendent Delphick in the past, so he naturally wants us on hand now. It's mostly Miss Seeton we're all counting on, though. She's a neighbor of ours in Kent, you know."

"So you aren't suspects at all, then.".

Meg smiled. "Don't look so disappointed. As you've explained to us, there are still several names on the list."

"Extraordinary young woman," Sir George said some time later, when he and Meg were taking the air on deck. "I mean, before all this happened, there she was drooping all over that frightful man. And then yesterday morning she looked like some grieving widow out of Alfred Lord Tennyson. Now all of a sudden she's full of the joys of spring, openly admitting she's glad to be shot of the bounder, and coming out with all this extraordinary stuff about everybody else. Jolly fishy, I call it . . . I say, come and look over here, what d'you make of that?''

Meg followed her husband over to the rail, and was in time to take in the scene that had caught her husband's eye. A police car had arrived on the quayside and drawn up at the foot of the gangway, where two uniformed Greek officers appeared to be urging a well-dressed, middle-aged man to board the *Eurydice*. He seemed to be in no hurry to do so, and was waving his arms about in an agitated way.

''D'you suppose Delphick's called for reinforcements? If so, they ought to get up here at the double, I'd say. That chap down there looks vaguely familiar, actually,'' Sir George was saying, when the Colvedens were joined at the rail by Miss Seeton and Dorcas. ''Oh, hello, you two. Been doing your physical jerks?''

''Sir George, sometime I'm going to sit you down and explain about yoga—what in the world is going *on* down there?'' Dorcas had begun speaking in measured, admonitory tones, but ended with an excited squeak. This was occasioned by the fact that the two policemen had suddenly seized the other man by the arms and were unceremoniously propelling him up the gangway.

''Why, it's Mr. Crivelli!'' Miss Seeton said.

''Why, so it is, George. We couldn't see his face till now,'' Meg added for the benefit of the new arrivals. ''He doesn't seem at all pleased to be back, does he?''

The gangway gave access to the deck below the one on which the four passengers were standing, and the struggling trio soon disappeared from view.

''I expect Mr. Delphick wants to talk to him,'' Miss

Seeton said. "If I might venture to say so, Dorcas dear, there would be little point."

"Point, Emily? In what?"

"In your explaining to Sir George about yoga. I have myself attempted—"

"Never mind that now, Miss Seeton! Tell us about this Crivelli fellow. I didn't put him on my list, you know. So why should Delphick have had him dragged back here kicking and screaming?"

"Well, I expect Mr. Delphick was struck by the coincidence, you see." Miss Seeton turned to Dorcas. "Lotto," she murmured, and after no more than a momentary pause the American's expression became one of complete understanding.

"Why, of *course*!" she cried. "Andrea Odoni! Emily, that's brilliant! But—"

"And naturally," Miss Seeton went on, "he would have questions for him, and he would probably want to consult his lawyers before replying. Mr. Delphick, that is. No, I mean Mr. Crivelli. To consult his lawyers before replying. To Mr. Delphick's questions. The one on the left has a nice little boy, by the way. He showed me a photograph last night."

"Well, I hope the poor child hasn't inherited his father's ears," Meg said. A veteran of many long conversations with Miss Seeton, she seldom had much difficulty in following her meaning, and had herself been struck by the fact that the Greek policeman's ears greatly resembled those of Prince Charles.

"I don't for the life of me understand what you're on about, Meg, nor how Miss Seeton got on to the Italian feller, but if you want to know my opinion, I think we should go and have a drink to celebrate. She's done it again, by Jove!"

"But, Sir George . . ." Colveden brushed aside Miss Seeton's mild protest.

"Yes, I know it's only just after eleven, but dash it all, you've solved another murder and I for one intend to drink your health. Oh, good, here comes old Wonky, he'll join me. Morning, Wonky, you're just in time to—good Lord, old boy, whatever's the matter? You look as if you've seen a ghost!"

chapter
~18~

"THANK YOU VERY much indeed, Miss Popjoy. And you, Mr. Taylor, for coming back for a second bite at the cherry. You've been enormously helpful. As I expect you know, Crivelli has been back on board for some time. We weren't going to broadcast the fact, but he created such a rumpus on arrival that he has nobody but himself to blame. I suppose it's too much to ask you to promise not to discuss this conversation with anyone else for a few hours?"

"I don't mind promising," Szabo said.

Juliana nodded. "Nor do I. Um, there is something else, Mr. Delphick, but it's . . . well, very confidential."

"Does it concern Crivelli?"

"No, not at all. Actually, Dickie and I did tell Amelita Forby about it. Has she said anything? We explained that we thought you ought to know, and that it would be easier for us if she'd pass it on to you."

"I see. Well, unless it's urgent, perhaps we should leave it like that for the moment at least. Captain Papagiannis and I really ought to see Crivelli now. You and I can have a private word later perhaps. If necessary."

Delphick rose courteously to his feet. If Juliana Popjoy had confided whatever it was on her mind to Mel, famous for her news scoops, it couldn't be anything so very explosive. Besides, it was nice to have an excuse to seek Mel out later on and ask her about it. Just the two of them. He took a step or two towards the door to open it for Juliana, but Papagiannis had beaten him to it, leaping out of his richly upholstered nest like a particularly frisky salmon and bowing low over Juliana's hand in the doorway while Szabo waited patiently behind her.

"That was interesting," Delphick said when he and Papagiannis had the cabin to themselves again.

"Very. And what a woman!" Papagiannis kissed his fingertips appreciatively. "Evidently, Crivelli is a crook. But is he also a murderer? And if so, how to prove it? There are no fingerprints on the murder weapon. And we cannot be so sure of the time of death to make any progress by checking alibis."

"No. Well, you weren't very keen on that idea anyway, were you? Look, I know you think I'm putting too much reliance on Miss Seeton's drawings, but in combination with what Taylor's just told us, I'm inclined to stick my neck out."

Papagiannis shrugged. "It is your neck," he said equably.

"So be it. I'm going to avoid a frontal assault. There's no need at this stage to accuse him of killing Witley. I'd prefer if possible to get him to convict himself of that out of his own mouth. Um, I wouldn't dream of suggesting that you should switch on that little tape recorder of yours. Your police regulations might be quite different from ours, after all. Mightn't they?"

"The reason I ask, George," Tump said, gazing glumly at the glass of pink gin he was nursing, "is that as a magistrate, you'll have come across a good many tricky situations. I mean, where a chap, basically a reasonably decent

sort of person I suppose, has some little weakness that puts
him into the sort of situation that, er, this friend of mine
finds himself in. Where he can't do the proper thing without
making it obvious to everybody that he has it. Er, the little
weakness I mentioned."

"Understand perfectly, old man. We had a policewoman
giving evidence in a case only a few months ago. Pleasant
young woman, married. She was in a big camera shop after
hours and caught a burglar in the act. Question arose, what
was she doing there in the first place? Well, she went as
red as a beetroot and asked if she could write it down. Can't
say I blame her, because it turned out she was with the shop
manager, both of them in the buff. They'd been having an
affair for some time, using the photographic studio upstairs,
and immortalising it in pictures. There was a sofa, apparently. It seems you can get these special cameras—"

"Yes, yes, I know."

"Anyway, the point is that since she made a clean
breast—bit unfortunate to put it like that, but you take my
meaning—since she spoke up honestly, or rather wrote it
down, the three of us on the Bench that day all kept mum,
and complimented her on doing her duty as a constable in
difficult circumstances. We never did find out what the
burglar made of it all."

Tump looked a little less miserable. "So you think this
friend of mine, if he were to do the right thing, might be
able to ask for his, er, weakness to be overlooked?"

"Guarantee it, old boy. Get it off your chest to me and
I'll put things right with Delphick . . . I mean, tell your
friend—oh, hang it all, Wonky, we all know about you
already, my dear chap, even that Welsh gel that talks like
a BBC announcer. So come on, out with it."

"For the last time, Mr. Crivelli, let me make it clear to
you that there isn't the slightest point in your persisting with

this show of outraged innocence,'' Delphick said wearily. ''Nor is it a bit of good pretending that you don't understand English. I have it on the authority of the captain of this ship and of several of your fellow passengers that you are virtually bilingual. Moreover, I repeat that my colleague Captain Papagiannis and I are at present carrying out a preliminary enquiry only. However, you are a man of the world. You can hardly suppose that your attitude today will have no bearing on the course of any formal proceedings in which you may find yourself involved.''

''I am under no obligation to answer any of your questions,'' Crivelli said sullenly. Delphick nodded slowly, gratified that the Italian had at last signalled his competence in English.

''That is true,'' Papagiannis agreed from the depths of his armchair. ''Also, you will have the right to remain silent even when charged.''

Crivelli whirled round and glared at the Greek officer. ''How dare you speak of charging me! If you have the impudence to imply that I murdered Adrian Witley, you'll live to regret it, I assure you. Let me tell you in any case that the moment I get out of here I shall instruct my Greek attorneys to sue you and your underlings for wrongful arrest, assault, and illegal imprisonment.'' He turned back to face Delphick again. ''And my legal advisers in London will take similar action there.''

''Oh, I wouldn't advise that, Mr. Crivelli. They're going to be quite busy enough defending you on serious fraud charges, quite apart from this matter of incitement to murder.''

''Fraud? Incitement to murder? What is all this, are you out of your mind?''

''When did you first meet Adrian Witley, Mr. Crivelli?''

''What sort of a question is that? I never set eyes on the man before the beginning of this cruise.''

"Rubbish," Delphick said mildly. "I'll put that question again in a minute, but before I do, let me explain one or two things to you. I am, as you know, concerned with criminal investigation work, and I am here because it is the job of the Metropolitan Police to look into serious crimes committed on board British ships, wherever they may be." Well, near enough, he thought to himself, and then mentally crossed his fingers. Miss Seeton had never let him down yet, and the message in her sketch of this wily fellow was pretty clear. He had to trust her to have got it right, and go out on a limb.

"My duties include the supervision of a team of specialist police officers who make it their business to find out how fake works of art find their way on to the international market. They are currently quite interested in a bust of Homer that was to have been auctioned at Sotheby's, but had to be withdrawn when its authenticity was questioned . . . when was it you said you first met the late Adrian Witley, Mr. Crivelli?"

"I . . . have corresponded with him. Over the years."

"Indeed you have. And with his Swiss bank."

"What are you suggesting?"

Delphick banged the writing table with both hands in exasperation. "For goodness sake, man, do you take me for an idiot? Suggesting? *Suggesting?* I'm telling you, Crivelli. I'm telling you that you have for years been in criminal association with Adrian Witley. That you, most likely with others, paid him to help you pass off spurious or dubious antiquities as being museum pieces of great value. By prostituting his high academic standing and scholarly reputation. And that such was Witley's status, you both got away with it, until a certain sharp-eyed dealer dared, like the little boy in the fable, to state that the emperor had no clothes. In other words, that the bust of Homer authenticated by Witley was a fake."

Crivelli sneered. "I know from personal experience how little the average ignorant English junk-shop owner knows about priceless works of art."

"If, as I suspect, you are alluding to the conspiracy you and Witley entered into to deceive Miss Juliana Popjoy about the true value of an amphora you bought from her, you can rest assured that we know all about that shabby trick. You look surprised: you shouldn't. Clever men like you often come unstuck as a result of assuming that everybody else is a fool. Mind you, you were right about Witley. He *was* a conceited fool, and as such had become dangerous to you. Your time was running out, Crivelli. You knew that in spite of Witley's loud talk about suing Szabo for defamation of character, he wouldn't. Because the Homer bust *is* a fake, and Szabo would be able to produce plenty of experts to prove it. And incidentally cast doubt on any number of other pieces bought in good faith by museums and collectors all over the world."

"That is why you told Witley to kill Szabo and make it look like an accident," Papagiannis said quietly, earning another venomous look from Crivelli, while Delphick sought further inspiration from the sketches on the table in front of him. He couldn't begin to fathom how Miss Seeton had unconsciously realised that so many people were all mixed up in this affair, but she had intuited their various roles and suggested them visually with uncanny accuracy.

In the Venus and Cupid sketch there was old Colveden presiding over all; as indeed he had, by engineering Miss Seeton's participation in the cruise in the first place, and later with his idiosyncratic but on the whole perfectly credible annotated list of suspects. The naked Venus with the face of Dorcas Bookbinder, and the enigmatic Pleasure figure of Blodwen Griffiths each threatened the rash Witley/Cupid, the one with an arrow, the other with her tail. It now seemed unlikely that either the ex-wife or the insulted mistress had killed Witley, but Miss Seeton's apparent faculty of precognition had led her to suggest even before his death that they might have had reason to.

Quite where Dickie Nash fitted in it was difficult to guess, but knowing Miss Seeton, she wouldn't have put him in the picture unless he had somehow impressed her as being involved. And finally the two masks, of comedy and tragedy. Well, judging by what Szabo had said about them, his misfortune in Venice and Witley's alleged attempt on his life in Corfu must have had their comic side; if only because Miss Seeton had been his saviour in both cases.

Wormclow Tump on the other hand was hardly a tragic figure. Pathetic in a way, perhaps, but that was because the laws of England affecting homosexual men were still barbaric. It looked as though there was a good prospect of their being changed before long, and provided Tump didn't come to grief before that happened, there was no reason why he shouldn't one day be freely accepted as what he was. At least he had powerful friends, not least George Colveden.

"Well, since you seem to have run out of baseless insinuations about me, how long do you two propose to hold me here against my will?"

Abruptly reminded where he was by the sound of Crivelli's voice, Delphick emerged from his reverie and stared at the man. In spite of his belligerent words, some of the fight had clearly gone out of him. Delphick openly picked up Miss Seeton's sketch of him as Andrea Odoni and held it up so that he could glance quickly from face to drawing and back again. It was interesting to compare them, and it also had the advantage of bothering Crivelli.

The Italian was, ostensibly at least, a collector of antiquities, and there he was in the drawing with a couple of small sculptures in the background, and some coins on a table in front of him—obviously a subtle if mysterious cross-reference to Blodwen Griffiths. Quite why Miss Seeton had seen fit to depict Crivelli in what looked like a fur-lined dressing gown was also a mystery, but of no importance whatever in the light of her truly astonishing feat in showing him holding in his hand a small statuette that closely resembled the weapon used to bludgeon Witley to death. How on *earth* could Miss S have predicted that?

Hang on, though, there was another puzzling item in the drawing. In the foreground at the foot Miss Seeton had suggested another couple of fragments of sculpture: what looked like the top half of a miniature version of the famous Venus de Milo, and a male head. Of some Roman or other, no doubt. But, Delphick asked himself, where the dickens had he seen that face before?

After a few seconds it came to him, and he addressed himself to Captain Papagiannis. "Captain, may I ask you to be so good as to summon a couple of your men to keep Mr. Crivelli company here for a while? Something else has cropped up that you and I ought to look into."

chapter
~19~

"WE'LL BE THERE in a minute or two," Captain Macallister said, and put the receiver of his internal telephone gently back into its cradle. Then he looked up from one to the other of the two senior police officers. "Come on," he then said grimly. "Ye'd better see for yourselves."

Delphick and Papagiannis exchanged glances: the Englishman's was expressionless, the Greek's puzzled. Then they followed the captain as he led the way into parts of the *Eurydice* normally never seen by passengers. They passed through heavy steel doors painted a dreary grey, through the surprisingly small galley, and into the crew's quarters beyond and below.

Pale of face, the purser was waiting for them outside a closed door. "Well," Macallister said to him. "Ye'll be hoping I'll not be sending ye tae any more cabins for a wee while. Open up."

The purser made no attempt to respond to the captain's sombre pleasantry, but took a passkey from his pocket and unlocked the door. Then he opened it an inch or two and stepped aside. It was Papagiannis who shoved it fully open and then stood stock-still, while Delphick and Macallister peered over his shoulders.

"I would have tried to cut him down, sir," the purser

said, audibly choking on the words. "If—"

"If it wasnae obvious that the poor boy's been dead some time. Fair enough, laddie. May the good Lord have maircy on his soul." Macallister turned away and put his arm round the purser's shoulders in a gesture of unexpected tenderness.

It was not the first time any of those present had seen a dead man, nor, in the case of the two policemen, the livid face and staring eyes of a man who had fairly obviously hanged himself. What made the spectacle of the steward Martin Hussingtree's dangling body peculiarly horrible even to those case-hardened men was the fact that the cabin was so tiny, and that they were therefore forced into close proximity to it.

"We must get him down," Delphick said, and without hesitation grasped the corpse around the thighs and hoisted it up. Papagiannis was a ready and effective partner. He scrambled up on to the narrow bunk, took a penknife from his pocket, and cut through the improvised noose—a colourful silk necktie—where it had been secured to a metal ceiling bracket. Then he jumped down and helped Delphick to lay the body on the bunk. It was Papagiannis who closed the eyes, took a hand towel from its rail at the side of the miniature metal washhand basin fixed to the bulkhead, and laid it over the ghastly face.

"Thank you," Delphick said to him. "Irregular, perhaps, before taking photographs, but in the circumstances . . ."

"Yes. You saw the notes too, I think. Not much doubt."

Delphick turned to Captain Macallister. "I think you can leave Captain Papagiannis and me to take the necessary steps and report to you later," he said, and then looked at the purser. "You've had an experience I wouldn't wish on anybody, and there's no need for us to distress you further by putting any questions to you for the present. We were with Captain Macallister when he rang to instruct you to find Hussingtree, and we heard you call him back to report no more than a few minutes later. So clearly you know as little as we do about all this."

"Ye'll be wanting the doctor here," Macallister pointed out.

"Yes, of course. You might perhaps be good enough to ask him to join us, oh, and one of the uniformed Greek police officers."

Macallister and the purser had been standing just outside the doorway, but even so there seemed to be more room to manoeuvre inside the cabin after they had gone. Papagiannis continued to impress Delphick, by producing a couple of clear plastic bags and a pair of tweezers from his seemingly inexhaustible trouser pockets. Using the tweezers, he picked up the two envelopes from the shelf on which they were propped, and inserted one into each bag. Then he passed them to Delphick to look at.

The envelopes were addressed in florid, rather childish handwriting adorned with extravagant curlicues. On one was written "His Excellency Sir Wormelow Tump"; on the other "Miss Emily D. Seeton."

"Can you slit them open with your knife without disturbing any dabs?" Delphick asked. "I'm afraid that as material evidence in a case of unnatural death they can't go directly to the addressees, and I don't really want to have to wait for your boys to dust them before I read them myself."

Papagiannis proved to be a deft hand with penknife and tweezers, and before long he had extracted from each envelope a single sheet of paper, folded once. When Papagiannis had teased open the first, Delphick bent over it. This is what he read:

Dear Sir Wormelow (I never thought that little me would ever have a Sir for a friend!!),
I am very sorry that I let you down, because you were

nice to me and, well, you know, you didn't put on airs
or anything. Being so important and all that. I know
I ought not to have taken Miss Seeton's pictures and
tried to get money off Professor (? spelling) Witley
and you and the horrible Italian. And I am at my wit's
end. So I must say sorry again and Goodbye, with love
from Marty. xxx.
P.S. We had a nice time, didn't we? Thanks a lot. M.

Delphick unaccountably found it necessary to blow his
nose violently before turning to the second note, which.
Papagiannis had now opened and which read:

Dear Miss S,
I am ever so sorry I stole your pictures and hit you I
never really wanted to hurt you but I was in such a
pickle and it was like a nightmare when I thought the
only way out was to kill you silly me. Anyway easier
said than done you are a bit of an Artful Dodger aren't
you. Mind you that Witley was asking for it if you
want my opinion, no regrets there. And I thought I
was being so clever going by your picture of old spa-
getti (?spelling) face and getting it blamed on him he
deserves it the lousy creep. Well Miss S I got thinking
I'd never outwit (good word!) "the Battling Brolly"
in person. You are a lot more use than me in this funny
old world anyway and besides you let me call you Miss
S. Not like some toffee nosed types. So it's Cheerio
and God Bless from me, and I want you to have my
Autograph Book.
With love from Marty. xxx
P.S. Bet you never get Larry Olivier's!!! M.

Delphick blew his nose again and reached for the autograph book on which Miss Seeton's letter had been standing.

To hell with the fingerprint man. He slipped it into his pocket and, without waiting for the ship's doctor to arrive, left Papagiannis to guard the body and deploy his specialists in due course.

Without too much difficulty he found his way back into the passenger area of the ship, and set out to give Captain Macallister a suitably edited account of the transformed state of the investigation brought about by Marty Hussingtree's suicide and the information contained in his two farewell letters, notably that addressed to Miss Seeton. The handwriting still had to be verified, but there was no doubt whatever in Delphick's mind that the young man had died by his own hand. Still moved by the brave jauntiness that showed through the banal, ill-turned phraseology of the letters, he was wondering what to do about them. Should the gist of the messages be conveyed to their intended recipients? If so, how and when?

It was a ticklish situation, so far as Tump was concerned, at least. Miss Seeton was emotionally quite robust enough to be given her letter neat, as it were. And come to think of it, there was no reason for delay. She could have a photocopy, until such time as the original could be released after being produced in evidence at the inquests on both Hussingtree and Witley; or whatever form of enquiry the Greeks and Scotland Yard eventually got around to agreeing on in the unusual circumstances. By giving Hussingtree's features to the Roman head in the foreground of her drawing of Crivelli, Miss Seeton had pointed the finger at him. Besides, she must receive her touching legacy from the steward without delay, and an explanation with it . . .

"Ah, there you are, Delphick! Been on the lookout for you, old man! Got a minute?"

Delphick blinked, shook his head, and became aware that he had reached the promenade deck, and that his way was being barred by Sir George Colveden.

"Ah, Sir George. Well, not just now, I'm afraid. I'm just on my way to see the captain—"

"Won't take a minute. I know how to be concise. Military training, you know. Besides, got to get back to the mems. Miss Seeton's teaching Meg how to stand on her head back there beside the swimming pool."

"Oh, very well. But make it snappy, please. I really am in a hurry." You can say that again, Delphick thought. Quite apart from everything else, that bloody man Crivelli's still cooling his heels with a couple of Greek coppers keeping an eye on him. Must decide what to do about him.

"Fact is, it's about old Tump. He came to me with a bit of a confession to make. It takes all sorts to make a world, you know, Delphick, and Wonky Tump isn't quite like you and me—"

"Sir George, I'm afraid I haven't time for a philosophical discussion with you. In any case, if you're telling me that Sir Wormelow is a homosexual, I've known that for years."

"You have? And you haven't hounded the fellow? Excellent. I've always thought of you as the sort of chap who'd turn a blind eye in the case of a harmless old boy like him. Anyway, the thing is, he's been a bit indiscreet, but in the process came by some vital information. About this murder, you know. Poor old Wonky's frightfully cut up about it. You'd better talk to him yourself, Delphick—what the devil's all that racket in aid of?"

The noise that had disturbed Colveden rapidly got louder and resolved itself into the pounding of booted feet, shouting in Greek, and occasional bumps and crashes as deck furniture was overturned. Then a single shot rang out, followed by an ominous silence. Delphick and Colveden were standing near a through walkway linking the two sides of the ship and were able to see what happened next. They saw Crivelli come briefly into view on the opposite side, backing past the gap, being stalked by two Greek policemen brandishing their revolvers.

Delphick was of course unarmed, but instinctively he set off on a parallel course, towards the stern of the ship, with Sir George puffing behind him. When he came to the end of the line of cabins that blocked the view of the other side, he peered cautiously round and was rewarded with a sight he would in more normal circumstances have savoured.

In the recreational area beside the tiny swimming pool were four ladies wearing tracksuits. Miss Seeton, who must surely have borrowed hers from Dorcas Bookbinder, had her head down, nestling between her forearms on a flat cushion. Her bottom was high in the air, and she was obviously about to kick herself up into the same sort of headstand already achieved by Dorcas, a few feet away from her. They were being watched with keen interest and perhaps a touch of apprehensiveness by Lady Colveden and Juliana Popjoy. All four had apparently been oblivious to the shot and remained blissfully unaware of the fact that they were being approached by an escaped suspect and two armed policemen.

Miss Seeton's timing was nevertheless perfect. Just as her feet shot up into the air Crivelli backed into them. He staggered sideways, Miss Seeton collapsed into his path, and Crivelli tumbled over her, straight into the pool.

chapter

~20~

"CAPTAIN PAPAGIANNIS, MAY I ask a favour of you?"

"Of course."

Delphick sat back in the deluxe cabin suite from which Crivelli had escaped only to be hauled, sodden and chastened, from the *Eurydice*'s swimming pool a few minutes later. Captain Macallister had been with them until a few minutes earlier, for a privileged sight of the draft preliminary report that Delphick and Papagiannis proposed to submit to their respective authorities.

Macallister had pointed out dourly that his own employers in London were going to want plenty of paperwork from him also, in the aftermath of the early termination of the *Eurydice*'s cruise at considerable consequential expense. Since he was going to have to report the death of one passenger, the arrest of a second, and the suicide of a member of the crew, the captain was grateful for the opportunity to ensure that his account of the circumstances would harmonize with the official police record.

"Well, this is going to be a nightmare for the bureaucrats to tidy up, especially at this end. Your people, the British Embassy, et cetera, et cetera," Delphick said.

Papagiannis raised his eyes heavenward and spread out his hands in an eloquent gesture. "You say so, I agree."

"But from our purely professional point of view, we seem to have got the facts reasonably straight and the situation under control."

"I suppose so. We have Crivelli in jail. A holding charge of obstructing the police in their duties, resisting arrest, exporting antiquities without licenses, and so on. We will enquire into his activities in Greece. In London you will prepare the proper indictment, and we will extradite him to you."

"Yes. We shall get him for major fraud, certainly. Incitement to murder, possibly. Crivelli is a lot less self-possessed than he was a few days ago, and it's always possible he might make a slip of the tongue under examination. Frank Taylor's likely to make an impressive witness—I shall always think of him as Ferencz Szabo, you know. Witley is hardly likely to have confided to Blodwen Griffiths that he was under Crivelli's orders to kill Szabo, but he could easily have said some careless things to her. She certainly knew about Witley's shady association with Crivelli."

"And the steward was a foolish amateur blackmailer who entered a game he was not qualified to play."

"Precisely. I'd say that Hussingtree was a bright, calculating young man, not well educated, but shrewd and with genuine charm. Certainly Miss Seeton liked him, and is very distressed by what has happened. She tells me that Hussingtree had read about her in the popular English papers and asked for her autograph the first time he brought her morning tea. That was when he happened to spot the most complex drawing she had made. She said she covered it up quickly, but presumably by then he'd recognised the faces of the passengers she had used as models. Later, as we know, he stole other drawings of hers. He confessed in his letters."

"And we found the drawings in his cabin."

"Stupidly, he tried to blackmail at least three people. Two of them were very bad choices."

"You think he showed the drawings to Witley and Crivelli?"

"Not to Witley, I think. A sketch of him as Cupid fondling the breast of a naked Venus who had been given the face of his former wife Dorcas Bookbinder would probably be more likely to have intrigued than embarrassed him. No, I think it's much more probable that Hussingtree hinted darkly to Witley that he knew certain secrets about him but would keep his mouth shut if paid; and that Witley jumped to the conclusion that Hussingtree had overheard one of his conversations with Crivelli. Given Witley's presumed state of mind, that would have been enough to throw him thoroughly off balance."

"But in that case Witley might have killed Hussingtree. Not the other way."

"True. But Witley might more simply have threatened to report the steward to the purser or even the captain, and get him fired. Crivelli, I should think, would have brushed Hussingtree off just as peremptorily, and again turned the threat back on him. So Hussingtree panicked, and concocted a scheme to silence Witley and at the same time frame Crivelli. He knew, you see, how much we in Scotland Yard value Miss Seeton's intuitive insights, and guessed that sooner or later I would spot the extraordinary resemblance between the little statuette she had shown Crivelli holding and the weapon used to kill Witley."

"No, Chief Superintendent. Here you lose me. It is impossible for me to believe that in his cabin, Witley just happened to have a Hercules statue similar to the one in Miss Seeton's picture."

"Ah, but I don't think he did, you see. Remember, we had only Hussingtree's own word for it that he had seen the statuette in Witley's cabin since the beginning of the voyage.

I think that having studied the drawing, Hussingtree went ashore and bought it. So does Miss Seeton, incidentally. She saw them on sale in a souvenir shop in Patmos, where the ship put in on the morning of Witley's death. Quite apart from that, why on earth would an expert like Witley want to put a cheap mass-produced thing like that on display? I'm afraid Hussingtree displayed his ignorance just when he was trying to be most cunning.''

Papagiannis shrugged. "There is a lot of, what do you call it, guesswork here. But we have the man's written confession in a suicide note, and we can believe it, I suppose. But what is this favour you spoke of some time ago?''

"We've come round quite neatly to it, actually, by mentioning the suicide note. The one to Miss Seeton. It contains all the essential points that will have to be brought out. The other one, to Sir Wormelow Tump, is in the truest sense personal. In it Hussingtree says nothing about killing Witley. He mentions having stolen the drawings and trying to blackmail the three men; but otherwise expresses nothing but high regard and touching affection for Sir Wormelow, and sincere regret for having, as Hussingtree put it, let him down. Unfortunately, it also makes it pretty clear that the two men had a brief but nonetheless homosexual relationship. Now I don't know how you view that sort of thing in Greece—''

"Dear colleague, surely you know it was considered to be elegant in classical times.'' Papagiannis smiled. "And don't you English still call it Greek love?''

"We used to. Anyway, I think you know what I'm about to suggest. Tump is a distinguished public figure, but more than that, he is a kindly and pleasant man. He could be ruined if it came out that he had dallied with a cabin steward. I'm proposing that we should quietly lose sight of the letter addressed to him, and forget we ever saw it.'' The Greek smiled again.

"I have no idea what letter you are talking about," he said blandly. "I remember no letter, and neither do my men."

"Thank you."

"Tell me, have you spoken to Tump about this?"

"No. But Sir George Colveden has, and I have every reason to believe that Tump was about to hazard his own position by volunteering a statement to me, before Hussingtree killed himself. But I was not available until it was too late. I shall make an opportunity to have a purely personal and private word with him later on."

"Well, I shall certainly take up the offer," Dorcas Bookbinder said firmly. "I'm longing to get off this ship and into a hotel, but I'm not through with Greece yet, and there are plenty of interesting places to visit by bus from Athens. I hope the rest of you are coming too."

"Mr. Treeves—he is the vicar of Plummergen, you know, would perhaps say that it's like the hymn. Through the night of doubt and sorrow, I mean."

"Onward go the pilgrim band," Sir George contributed in an unexpectedly pleasing baritone. "Singing songs of umpty umpty, *tumpty* tumpty promised land. Absolutely, Miss Seeton. Greece was what I promised to Meg, and so did the Halcyon Holiday people. We're all going, I take it?"

With the exception of Sir Wormelow Tump, all the remaining passengers, plus Mel Forby, were sitting in a companionable circle in the main lounge over drinks.

Blodwen Griffiths nodded agreement. "I am. Do you mind if I hang around with you people?"

"That would be a pleasure, dear," Meg Colveden said. "Frank?"

"Of course. Count me in. I rather fancy I've been on my

last cruise, but if Miss Seeton promises to watch over me I'll take a chance on dry land.''

"Would Dickie and I be in the way?" Juliana enquired.

Sir George beamed at her. "Good heavens no! By the way, Nash, I owe you some money.''

"Me? Surely not.''

"Oh, yes I do. I offered a hundred to one that a CID man would come and sort all this nonsense out in a brace of shakes, and you wagered a tenner. But it was really Miss Seeton who turned up trumps in the end. I take it my check will be acceptable?''

An awed silence fell as Sir George pulled out a check book from his inside pocket.

"A *thousand pounds*? No, no, you didn't mean it seriously. I couldn't possibly—''

"Nonsense! It was a fair bet, with plenty of witnesses—''

"Wait a minute, Sir George.'' Mel spoke quietly, but something about her manner compelled attention. "I think it's handsome of you to pay out, and I think Dickie should accept. On one condition. That he recognises that it was the last money wager he'll ever make.''

There was a long silence, during which Dickie Nash reached for Juliana's hand. Then he grinned happily.

"Done!'' he said.

Delphick and Mel were standing at the rail, talking quietly, when a Greek policeman approached, saluted smartly, and handed Delphick a sealed envelope, marked "PERSONAL: Chief Superintendent Delphick.'' "From Captain Papagiannis,'' the policeman said carefully in English. Then he saluted again, made a little bow towards Mel, and retreated. Delphick ripped the envelope open and took out Marty Hussingtree's letter addressed to Tump, still in the plastic bag in which Papagiannis had replaced it after they had both read it. Attached to the plastic was a short note:

> Dear Colleague: Please dispose of this as you wish. My compliments and respects to you and to the charming Miss Forby.
>
>   X. Papagiannis

"Papagiannis sends you his compliments and respects, Mel."

"How nice. What's that in the bag?"

"Oh, something I need to have a word with Wormelow Tump about."

They both turned and looked toward the spare figure of Tump, who was standing alone at the very back of the ship, his back turned to them. "He looks so lonely and sad," Mel said. "Why didn't he go to the hotel with the others?"

"I think he's decided to go straight back to London on the evening plane. Do you mind if I go and talk to him for a minute now, Mel? What I have to tell him—and give him—might cheer him up a little."

"Of course not. And what after that?"

"Well, after that, if you can square your editor with a splendid exclusive about the Battling Brolly, and if I can persuade Sir Hubert Everleigh that I need a few days more in Greece to sort everything out, I suggest that you and I might avail ourselves of the hospitality of Halcyon Holidays. They are two passengers short, after all. And I'd specially like to visit Delphi."

"Why Delphi in particular?"

Delphick smiled at her, and Mel knew what he was going to say before he said it.

"What do you think they call me the Oracle for?"